I0643245

THE WEREWOLF

HIS SCIENCE AND PRACTICE

By

MONTAGUE SUMMERS

This edition published by Read Books Ltd.
Copyright © 2019 Read Books Ltd.
This book is copyright and may not be
reproduced or copied in any way without
the express permission of the publisher in writing

British Library Cataloguing-in-Publication Data
A catalogue record for this book is available
from the British Library

Initiati sunt Beelphegor: et comederunt
sacrificia mortuorum.
Et immolauerunt filios suos, et filias suas dæmoniis.
Et effuderunt sanguinem innocentem. Et fornicati sunt
in adinuentionibus suis

Psalm cv

CONTENTS

MONTAGUE SUMMERS

Augustus Montague Summers was born in Bristol, England in 1880. He was raised as an evangelical Anglican in a wealthy family, and studied at Clifton College before reading theology at Trinity College, Oxford with the intention of becoming a Church of England priest. In 1905, he graduated with fourth-class honours, and went on to continue his religious training at the Lichfield Theological College. Summers entered his apprenticeship as a curate in the diocese of Bitton near Bristol, but rumours of an interest in Satanism and accusations of sexual misconduct with young boys led to him being cut off; a scandal which dogged him his whole life. Summers joined the growing ranks of English men of letters interested in medievalism and the occult. In 1909, he converted to Catholicism and shortly thereafter he began passing himself off as a Catholic priest, the legitimacy of which was disputed. Around this time, Summers adopted a curious attire which included a sweeping black cape and a silver-topped cane.

Summers eventually managed to make a living as a full-time writer. He was interested in the theatre of the seventeenth century, particularly that of the English Restoration, and was one of the founder members of The Phoenix, a society that performed neglected works of that era. In 1916, he was elected a fellow of the Royal Society of Literature. Summers also produced some important studies of Gothic fiction. However, his interest in the occult never waned, and in 1928, around the time he was acquainted with Aleister Crowley, he published the first English translation of Heinrich Kramer and James Sprenger's *Malleus Maleficarum* ('*The Hammer of Witches*'), a 15th century Latin text on the hunting of witches. Summers then turned to vampires, producing *The Vampire: His Kith and Kin* (1928) and

The Vampire in Europe (1929), and then to werewolves with *The Werewolf* (1933). Summers' work on the occult is known for his unusual, archaic writing style, his intimate style of narration, and his purported belief in the reality of the subjects he treats.

In his day, Summers was a renowned eccentric; *The Times* called him "*in every way a 'character'*" and "*a throwback to the Middle Ages.*" He died at his home in Richmond, Surrey.

HIS SCIENCE AND PRACTICE

THE Common Wolf (*Canis lupus*), says St. George Mivart in his monograph *Dogs, Jackals, Wolves, and Foxes,*[1] " is the largest and most dreaded of the Canidae," a family which is one of several others making up the " Order " of " Beasts of Prey " or *Carnivora*. The wild Canidae are distributed over the greater part of the habitable globe, in the Old World from Spitzbergen and Siberia to the Cape of Good Hope and Java, in the New World from Arctic shores to Tierra del Fuego and the Falkland Islands.

The European wolf may be considered as the survivor of a group of ferocious beasts of prey, the cave-bear, the cave-hyena, and others, the fiercest enemies of prehistoric man. Although extinct in Great Britain and Ireland, the wolf still exists in some numbers in the west of the continent of Europe, in the wilder and more mountainous parts of France, Belgium (Forest of Ardennes), Hungary, East Prussia, Austria (Carinthia), and very abundantly in Russia.[2]

The size and proportions of the wolf roughly resemble those of a large mastiff dog, although individuals, particularly from different localities, differ very greatly in size, and the Russian variety especially attains most powerful dimensions. The prevailing colour is a tawny or rufous grey, and the greyness is apt to increase with age. The head, back of the neck, shoulders, loins, and crupper are blackish with yellow tints. There is a very thick and dense underfur of a slate or brown colour, intermixed with whitish and black-tipped hairs. The thighs and outsides of the legs are reddish yellow, varying to a darker brown ; the tail is full, of medium length, dark brown above and lighter below, and tipped with black. The inner side of the limbs is of a dirty yellowish grey. The lower jaw, the margin of the upper jaw, the inside of the ear, and the belly are more or less white. The exterior of the ears is usually dark brown and covered with short velvety fur ; whilst the whiskers are black and few in number.

The teeth are sharp-cutting blades of great strength. This is also noted by Ricchieri, who in his *Lectiones Antiquae*, Liber xxi, c. 24, comments upon a passage in the third *Georgic*, ll. 206–8 :—

> namque ante domandum
> ingentes tollent animos, prensique negabunt
> verbera lenta pati, et duris parere lupatis.

" Quo in loco Servius, et qui abeo mutuati sunt plures, esse lupata tradunt frena asperrima, sic de lupinorum dentium similitudine nuncupata, quos esse inaequales constet, unde et morsus infigatur summi nocumenti." Ulisse Aldrovandi, also, in his *De Quadrupedibus Solidipedibus* has much to say of the " lupata frena ".[3]

" The English wolf," remarks Poland, " was undoubtedly very much of the above description, but of smaller size and darker colour, and was also probably of a fierce disposition." [4]

Wolves frequent both forests and open country, and they are to be encountered by day as well as night, either singly, in pairs, or in packs.   In severe and cold winter weather they leave their coverts and assemble in herds for predatory purposes.   The packs will thus even penetrate into villages. It has been estimated that in 1875 161 persons fell victims to wolves in Russia, and in 1878 the damage to cattle was estimated at seven and a half millions of roubles.   Wolves destroy horses and herds by combined attacks for the most part, but they will singly destroy sheep, goats, and children. They greedily devour birds, and will eat mice, frogs, or almost any small animals.   They also feed on carrion, and are said to seek nourishment from buds and lichens.

The voice of the wolf is unmistakable, a long-drawn howl of peculiar and most eerie quality.   Wolves in confinement will learn to bark if they hear dogs do so.

The males fight together in January, the successful combatant obtaining a female with whom he remains until the young are advanced in growth.   " He goeth to rut in the whole yeere not above twelve daies," says Pliny of the wolf in his *Natural History*, viii, 22.[5]

Throughout the ages, even in the prehistoric world, whilst his howling athwart the stillness of nature and night struck fear into the heart of primaeval man crouching far back in the dark retreat of some cold rough cave ; further down the centuries when he was known as the savage plunderer and swift pitiless marauder of the shepherd's grazing flocks, not sparing to attack child and maid or even the solitary way-farer by the wood ; nearer yet, what time the red glare of his eyes across a drear plain of unflecked snow in the cold steely moon has paralyzed some lonely leash of travellers, and the plunging horses mad with terror break into a frenzied gallop, their unchecked career whirling the heavy sleigh as a mere straw-weight jerry-jingle behind, whilst the gaunt shadowy forms muster in a greater company and advance with fearful rapidity towards their human prey ; all down the vistas of dateless centuries the wolf has ever been the inevitable, remorseless enemy of man, and few animals indeed has the world's fancy, nay, the experience and dearly purchased knowledge of our forefathers, invested and surrounded with so many gloomy superstitions and beliefs that are horribly real and true.

The distinctive features of the wolf are unbridled cruelty, bestial ferocity, and ravening hunger. His strength, his cunning, his speed were regarded as abnormal, almost eerie qualities, he had something of the demon, of hell. He is the symbol of Night and Winter, of Stress and Storm, the dark and mysterious harbinger of Death.

In Holy Writ the wolf is ever the emblem of treachery, savagery, and bloodthirstiness.[6] Our Lord, indeed, in the New Testament uses words than which nothing could be darker and more condemnatory. The wolf is the type of the heretic. "Beware of false prophets, who come to you in the clothing of sheep, but inwardly they are ravening wolves," S. Matthew, vii, 15. Again, to His disciples He said in the solemn moment when He delivered that great charge and gave them power over unclean spirits, to cast them out : "Behold I send you as sheep in the midst of wolves," S. Matthew, x, 16. The Good Shepherd spoke of the sorrows and tribulations which were to fall upon His Church : "But the hireling, and he that is not the shepherd, whose own the sheep are not, seeth the wolf coming, and leaveth the sheep, and fleeth : and the wolf catcheth, and scattereth the sheep," S. John, x, 12. S. Paul also, in his sad farewell, took up Our

Lord's words : " I know that, after my departure, ravening wolves will enter in among you, not sparing the flock," Acts, xx, 29.

The evening wolves, says the learned Cornelius a Lapide, are demons, who verily prowl abroad in the dark hours, and urge man to every kind of lust and murder, and to other infinite crimes.[7]

Certes there is in the divine phrase something more than a suggestion of the demoniacal nature of the wolf. He stands not merely for the murderer of the body, that were perhaps a light thing ; but what is infinitely worse, as S. Ambrose tells us,[8] he typifies the heretic, the murderer of the soul.

In Early English use the word Wolf is applied to the Devil (wolf of hell) and his agents, as by Chaucer in the *Persones Tale* (c. 1386) : " As seith seint Augustyn, they been the deueles wolues that stranglen the sheepe of Ihesu crist." In the *Godstow Register*, Kalendar, 18 June, there is an invocation, " Cyryce and Iulytte kepe us fro the wulfe ! " (Satan). Bishop Alcock in his *Mons Perfectionis* (A iij) has : " It putteth from as the wulf the deuyll deuourer of mannes soul " ; whilst as late as 1577 Kendall, in his *Flowers of epigrammes*, speaks of " The feend the woulfe of hell ! "[9]

In classical authors the wolf[10] is the eternal symbol of ferocity and inordinate evil appetite, hard by which rides cruel devouring lust. The desire of blood and the desire of flesh are found to be never far apart. A smock-faced amoroso in Aristaenetus complains of the vampirish lechery of some old unsatisfied dowager who dry-founders him till he has fallen to a mere sapless keck. " Ods my life," he cries, " these men-leeches,[11] hags, love a youngling just like wolves, and in sooth their cravings are the venery of the she-wolf on heat " (λυκοφιλία).[12]

Plato, in the *Phaedrus*,[13] " ὦ παῖ, ξυννοεῖν, καὶ εἰδέναι τὴν ἐραστοῦ φιλέαν, ὅτι οὐ μετ' εὐνοίας γίγνεται, ἀλλὰ σιτίου τρόπον, χάριν πλησομενῆς, ὡς λύκοι ἄρν' ἀγαπῶσ', ὡς παῖδα φιλοῦσιν ἐρασταί."

Remember, my beautiful boy, that a lover's passion is not unselfish, but he thirsts to accomplish his desire. For

The eager lover to the boy aspires,
Just as the wolf the tender lamb desires.[14]

And Strato writes an epigram [15] :—

Νυκτερινὴν ἐπίκωμος ἰὼν μεταδόρπιον ὥρην
ἄρνα λύκος θυρέτροις εὗρον ἐφεσταότα,
υἱὸν ᾿Αριστοδίκου τοῦ γείτονος· ὃν περιπλεχθεὶς
ἐξεφίλουν ὅρκοις πολλὰ χαριζόμενος.
νῦν δ᾿αὐτῷ τί φέρων δωρήσομαι; οὔτ᾿ ἀπάτης γὰρ
ἄξιος ῾Εσπερίης οὔτ᾿ ἐπιορκοσύνης.

> By night, on pleasure bent, my dinner o'er,
> Like to a wolf, I came before the door
> Of Aristòcidus, and then I saw
> His lamb-like son, and unto him I swore
> To give him many gifts, and plighted troth
> To him with kisses twain ; now am I loath
> To disappoint the boy ; as if my oath
> Of wine-bred fancy were indeed the growth.[16]

Thus λύκος was sometimes applied to a homosexual lover. Pollux in his *Onamasticon* [17] lists among the Comic Masks τὸ λυκαίνιον, the wolfish mask. This was worn by the lewd old trot whose face was raddled by wrinkles and ghastly pale, whilst none the less she ogled and was an adept in giving " the languishing Eye, as they call it, that is the Whitings-Eye, of old called the Sheeps-Eye ". In the Orphic Hymns Λύκαινα is an epithet of Aphrodite.[18] It is possible that from this Greek Mask τὸ λυκαίνιον was derived the Latin term *lupa*, literally a she-wolf, but meaning a bulker, a common dirty whore. Pierre Pierrugues, in his *Glossarium Eroticum Linguae Latinae*,[19] gives the derivation of *lupa* from the wolf, since that animal goes prowling abroad after its prey. In the *Truculentus* [20] Strabax has a pun on the original meaning : " Nam oveis illius haud longe absunt a lupis."

Lactantius, *De falsa religione*, i, 20, thus explains the tradition that Romulus and Remus were suckled by a she-wolf (*lupa*). He says that Larentia, the wife of the shepherd Faustulus, who found the babes, and the nurse of Romulus, was commonly named Lupa (whore) because she would shamelessly lie down to any rustic who solicited her. Hence arose the legend that a she-wolf was the foster mother of Rome's founder. " Romuli nutrix Lupa honoribus est affecta divinis. Et ferrem si animal ipsum fuisset, cujus figuram gerit, Auctor est Livius, Larentiae esse simulacrum, et quidem non corporis, sed mentis, ac morum. Fuit enim

Faustuli uxor, et propter vulgati corpore vilitatem, Lupa inter pastores, id est meretrix nuncupata est ; unde etiam Lupanar [bawdy-house] dicitur." He then refers to the statue of a lioness erected by the Athenians to Leæna,[21] an Athenian hetaera, who is connected with the story of Harmodius and Aristogeiton. These two lovers killed the brother of the tyrant Hippias, Hipparchus, who offered violence to the young and comely Harmodius. Harmodius was cut down, and Aristogeiton, escaping for a while, when captured expired under tortures. Athens reverenced them as martyrs and the saviours of their country. Their example, moreover, consecrated, as it were, homosexual love, and their two names became eponyms of paiderastia.[22] To do them public honour their statues, cast in bronze by Antenor, were set up in the Agora. Leæna, whose actual part in the history does not seem very clear, was put to the question as being privy to the affair, but she died under her sufferings without making any disclosure, and (as it is said) she bit off her tongue that no secret might be wrung from her. She was honoured by a bronze statue of a lioness (λέαινα) without a tongue, which was set up on the Acropolis between the Propylaea and the temenos of Artemis Brauronia.[23]

The word *lupa* is frequent in Latin authors. The Scholiast on Juvenal, iii, 66, glosses on *picta lupa* " meretrices ",[24] and upon the phrase of Ausonius, Epigram., xxvi, 12, " Et mater est vere lupa," Vinetus comments : " Scortum. Meretricum enim mores, voraci luporum ingenio, haud sunt dissimiles. Alludit autem ad fabulam de Romulo et Remo a lupa lactatis, apud Livium, Plutarchum, Halicarnasseum." [25] Prudentius, *adversus Symmachum*, i,[26] has of Priapus :—

> Scortator nimius, multaque libidine suetus
> Rusticulas vexare lupas, interque salicta
> Et densas sepes obscoena cubilia inire.

In the famous work of Nicolas Chorier, which is generally known under the title *Aloisia Sigœa Toletana De arcanis Amoris et Veneris* (Joannis Meursii, *Elegantiae Latini Sermonis*),[27] Colloquium vi, " Veneres," the erudite Tallia discourses : " Lupae sunt et meretrices, quae, nulla voluptatis habita ratione, pretio merent, aut merere vulgo audiunt, putidae, e misera et jejuna plebecula. Quo cumque protervae se tulerint, lupanaris secum sordes invehent. Ignominiosum ipsae sunt sibi opprobrium . . . Lupa et lupanar inventa sunt vocabula ad ignominiam fortunae, non morum."

From *lupa* we have the cognate words *lupana*, a whore ; *lupatria*, a strumpet ; *lupari*, to fornicate or wimble ; *lupanar*, also *lupanarium*, a brothel-house ; *lupanarius*, a cock-bawd ; and the adjective *lupanaris*, lascivious, lewd.

In Italian *lupo* is sometimes used to designate a lecher, as by Giovanni Rucellai in his tragedy *Rosmunda*,[28] Acto terzo, where the Nurse says :—

> Ma queste nostre misere fanciulle
> Darai in preda ad affamati lupi,
> Ch'insio nel grembo dell'afflitte madri
> Verranno ad isfogar le voglie loro.

Lupa also designates a whore ; for example, Segneri in his *Prediche*, v, 9, has : " Come dunque scialaequar prima la vostra robatra parasiti, tra buffoni, e tra lupe, che darla a Cristo." *Lupanaio, lupanario,* and *lupanare* all signify a brothel-house. Segneri, *Prediche*, viii, 6 : " V'invita a feste [il compagno] v'invita a festini, v'invita a balli, v'invita sin tal volta a luoghi infamissimi, a lupercali, a postriboli, a lupanari."

In *Acolastus*, iv, 6, the unhappy prodigal soliloquizes :—

> o dolor, dolor.
> Vt dij uos male perdant lupae obscoenissimae
> Quibus seruiui turpiter.

Upon which John Palsgrave in his interpretation of the comedy writes : " O sorowe, sorowe, i.o. redoubled sorowe, or o sorow upon sorowe that euyl mought the goddes lose you, o you most uggly or abhomynable she wolfes, whom I haue vily serued. i. that I beseche god send you an euyll myschefe, you moste lothesome cutte tayled bytches, whom I haue become slaue unto, thus shamefully. (*Comparatio Lupae i. scorti ad lupam.*) But yet is there a more vehemēce comprysed by the auctour, to lyken myswomen unto she wulfes, as dyuerse latine auctours doo testyfie, and Jehan de Meun, in his frenche Romant of the rose." [29]

Death walked hand in hand with lust, and we may note that in an old Etruscan vase-painting Charon, the ferryman of hell, is wrapped in a wolf's fur.[30] The omen of the wolf was unlucky in the highest degree. He carries disappointment, disaster, and doom.[31]

Lust, then, as well as blood is associated with the wolf.

Giambattista della Porta, physician, philosopher, and cabbalist, who was born in 1540 and died in 1615, tells us that in his day the country folk of the kingdom of Naples still fixed over the door of their huts a wolf's head with wide gaping jaws to defend from sorcerers and witches; they still held that the skin from a wolf's neck was a most powerful periapt. Moreover, they believed that a man who trenchered succulently on roast wolf's flesh would be immune from the frauds and molestations of goblin, evil spirits, bogle, and incubi. Wolf's flesh roast and minced with other food was a sovran remedy for black melancholy.[32]

Thus Mr. Frank Cowper in his stirring and well-told novel, *Cædwalla, or The Saxons in the Isle of Wight*, just before the night attack on Cissanceaster, when the warriors are startled for a moment at the unearthly screech, imagining it is some foul sorceress yelling to her kind, makes old Ceolwulf volunteer and say: " Atheling, I will go, I have no fear of witches ; I have a wolf's snout hung round my neck, and no witch can hurt me, be her charms never so powerful." [33]

Girolamo Cardano in his *De Subtilitate Libri XXI*, first published in 1550,[34] writes that a wolf's tail hung up in a stable or byre, entirely prevents the horses or the oxen from eating. Horses treading in a wolf's soreth are mazed and founder. They snuff the foe. The head of a wolf suspended in a pigeon house has virtue to protect any columbary from the attack of ferrets or weasels. He will not, however, vouch that the chape of a wolf, if buried, keeps off the annoyance of gnats and flies. A mash of the intestines, skin and treddles of the wolf cureth colicky gripes. But Cardano doubts whether, as some aver, a wolf's pizzle, dried and minced, when eaten will prove a potent aphrodisiac.[35]

" It is commonly thought," says Pliny, treating of wolves, " and verily beleeved, that in the taile of this beast, there is a little string or haire that is effectuall to procure love, and that when he is taken at any time, hee casteth it away from him, for that it is of no force and vertue unless it be taken from him whiles he is alive." [36]

Leonard Vair, also, in his *De Fascino*, i, 8, remarks : " Lupi etiam caudae exiguo in villo, amatorium virus inesse credit, qui si viuenti non detrahatur, vim nullam habere refert." [37]

It is not well even to dream of a wolf, so Artemidorus in his *Oneirocritica*,[38] ii, 12, instructs us : " Λύκος δὲ ἐνιαυτὸν σημαίνει διὰ τὸν λυκάβαντα, τοῦτ' ἐστι, τὸν χρόνον ; ὡς οἱ ποιηταὶ ὀνομάζουσιν ἀπὸ τοῦ περὶ τὰ ζῶα ταῦτα συμβεβηκότος. Ἀεὶ γὰρ ἑπόμενα ἀλλήλους ἐν τάξει δίεισι τὸν ποταμόν, ὥσπερ αἱ τοῦ ἔτους ὧραι ἑπόμεναι ἀλλήλαις τελοῦσι τὸν ἐνιαυτόν. Καὶ ἔχθρὸν δὲ βίαιόν τινα καὶ ἁρπακτικόν, καὶ πανοῦργον, καὶ ἐκ τοῦ φανεροῦ ὁμόσε χωροῦντα."

Seldom, very seldom, is the wolf lucky. Pliny, however, gives us the exception. " In the case of presages and fore-tokens of things to come, this is observed, that if men see a wolfe abroad, cut his way and turne to their right hand, it is good ; but if his mouth be full when he doth so, there is not a better signe nor more luckie in the world again." [39]

Aristophanes of Byzantium, also, *Historiae Animalium Epitome*,[40] ii, 242, tells us of the virtue of a wolf's tooth : πύκου δ' ὄδοντα τις ἐξαψέμονος τοῦ αὐχένος, ἀδεῶς ἂν τοῖς ὁμοφύλοις ἐντύχῃ θηρίοις. His epithet for the wolf is the significant ἄδικος.

Aubrey, *Remaines of Gentilisme and Judaisme*, remarking upon amulets and corals, says : " The Irish doe use a woolves fang-tooth set in silver for this purpose ; which they hold to be better than coral. And in the very same manner the children in Germany weare about them furnished too with little silver bells." Again, he notes : " Coralls are worne by children still ; but in Ireland they value the fang-tooth (holder) of an wolfe before it : which they set in silver and gold as we doe yᵉ Coralls." [41]

The following is an old Sicilian pastoral wolf-charm : " Per ligari li lupu pignia una strinza di dainu oï capriu e non voi mangiari carni allupata. Santu Silvestru a munte oliveri stava, la sua bistiami pascia e guardava, scisi fera di boscu, quali mangiau, quali pulicau, quali a mmala via li mandau. Santu Silvestru a menzu la via stava e plangia e lacrimava : Jesu Christu et la virgi Maria passava dissi li : Chi ai, Silvestru, chi planzi e llagrimi ? Oï, signuri comu non vognu plangiri e lagrimari ? A munti oliveri stava la mia bistiami, pascia e guardava, scisi fera di boscu quali mangiau, quali pulicau, quali a mmala via li mandau." " Silvestru, per ki non li ligi ? Signuri, chi mi lùgu chi non saggiu, nesci la sira poichi scura, e ddi perchi la stidda una chi luggi piu chi lluna e dal lupu e uligu denti e ad uni animali chi pitterra strascina ventri chi non faccia mali ala mia bistiami pedi giaccatu non perdir ritundu per fina chi lu suli non giungi ala tavul di lu santu Salvaturi.   Allaudi di Jesu Christu eddila virgini Maria dirremu un paternostru ed una avi Maria. Ariel sichar lormai emanuel sutiel con juru vos spiritus praenominatus per alpha et o et per principem vestrum sosolimo ut quam oculus meus viderit, uti conrumpere faciatis visa ut ineat amorem meum." [42]

There is a seemingly world-wide and most ancient tradition concerning the wolf, which, since I am unable to decide upon the truth of the matter, will perhaps best be treated by reference to a quota of authorities and others noticing it in their writings. Accordingly I will cite in the first place— inasmuch as he so concisely in his well-flavoured trenchant English sums up the point—Dr. George Hakewell, who says in his *Apologie or Declaration of The Power and Providence of God in the Government of the World*, book i, chapter i, sect. v, 9 (folio, Oxford, 1627 and again 1635) [43] : " That a *Woolfe* if he see a man first suddenly strikes him dumb, whence came the proverbe *Lupus est in fabula*, and that of the poet :—

> *Lupi Mœrim videre priores,*
> The Wolues saw Mœris first.

" Yet *Phillip Camerarius* (*Meditat. Histor. cap.* 28) professes, *fabulosam esse quod vulgo creditur, nominem à lupo prœuisum subitò consternari & vocem amittere,* That it is fabulous which is commonly beleeued that a man being first seene by the Woolfe is therevpon astonished and looseth his voyce ; And that himselfe hath found it by experience to be a vaine opinion, which *Scaliger* (*Exercitat.* 344) likewise affirmes vpon the same ground. *Vtinam tot ferulis castigarentur mendaciorum assertores isti quot à Lupis visi sumus sine jactura vocis.* I wish those Patrons of lies were chastised with so many blowes as at sundry times I haue beene seene of woo/ues without any losse of my voyce."

The most celebrated allusion to this belief is contained in Vergil's ninth Eclogue, 53–4 :—

> vox quoque Moerim
> iam fugit ipsa ; lupi Moerim videre priores.

which Dryden Englishes thus :—

> My Voice grows hoarse ; I feel the Notes decay,
> As if the Wolves had seen me first to Day. [44]

18

Servius in his Commentary on this passage of Vergil glosses : " hoc etiam physici confirmant, quod voce deseretur quem prior viderit lupus."

Theocritus, also, xiv, 22, has :—

" οὐ φθεγξῇ ; λύκος εἶδέ σ' ; " ἐπαιξέ τις. " ὡς σοφός " εἶπε, κἠφᾶπτ'.

" Won't you speak ? Has a wolf seen you ? " jested some quiz, " as the wise man said."

Plato, although not precisely mentioning the old belief, refers to it in the First Book of the *Republic*, when Thrasymachus has interrupted the discussion in a loud blustering voice, and Socrates declares : " I was astonied beyond measure, and gazed at the speaker in terror ; and methinks if I had not set eyes on him before he eyed me, I should verily have been struck dumb."

We now approach a very important point in the study of the Werewolf. When a man is metamorphosed into a wolf, or into any other animal form whatsoever it may be, is there an actual, corporeal, and material change, or else is the shape-shifting fantastical, although none the less real and substantially apparent to the man himself and to those who behold him ; and if it be thus simulated and illusory how is the phenomenon accomplished ?

The famous Jean Bodin, who devotes the sixth chapter of the second book of his *De la Demonomanie des Sorciers* (Paris, 1580) to a study of lycanthropy—*De la Lycanthropie et si le Diable peut changer les hommes en bestes* [45]—gives it as his opinion that the demon can really and materially metamorphose the body of a man into that of an animal, only he cannot change and alter the human understanding. Bodin argues for a substantial change, and quotes in his support S. Thomas Aquinas : *Omnes Angeli boni et mali ex uirtute naturali, habent potestatem transmutandi corpora nostra.*[46] " Or si nous confessons que les hommes ont bien la puissance de faire porter des roses à vn cerisier, des pommes à vn chou, & changer le fer en acier, & la forme d'argent enor, & faire mille sortes de pierres artificielles, qui côbatent les pierres naturelles, doibt on trouuer estrange, si Sathan change la figure d'vn corps en l'autre, veu la puissance grande que Dieu luy donne en ce monde elemêtaire."

There are, it is true, other learned and weighty writers who have maintained that (under God) the Devil has power actually to change a human being corporeally into a wolf or some other animal, but it was Bodin who was universally regarded and so violently attacked as the chief exponent of this argument. His chapter is of prime importance in the history of the philosophical conceptions of lycanthropy, and demands a particular examination.

He commences by emphasizing the fact that the transvection of witches to the sabbat, although sometimes fantastical, since the witch lies in a trance whilst psychically she assists at Satan's synagogue, is also oftener material, and she travels thither bodily conveyed. The Devil deludes her so that she imagines she is carried by the power of some muttered words or by the force of the sorcerers' unguent. At these orgies the demon generally appears to the assembly in the form of a huge he-goat. Sometimes he shows himself as a tall dark man.

It is a wonderful thing that the Devil should be able to change a man into a beast. Yet in the *Malleus Maleficarum* we read of a certain leader of witches (part ii, qn. i, ch. 15) [47] named Staufer, who lived in Berne, and whose boast it was that he could change himself into a mouse and thus slip through the hands of his enemies. He left two disciples, Hoppo and Stadlin, who could raise violent hailstorms.

Bodin then rehearses in some detail the case of Gilles Garnier, condemned and executed for lycanthropy at Dole, 18th January, 1583, and refers to the trial of Pierre Burgot and Michel Verdun, two notorious werewolves, in 1521. He also cites the instance of the lycanthrope of Padua, as described by Job Fincel [48]; and the coven of witches who under the form of cats met in the old haunted castle of Vernon. When some of these animals had been wounded, certain old women were found hurt in exactly the same place on their bodies. There is also the example of the wood-chopper who lived in a town not far from Strasburg. Whilst hewing faggots this man was attacked by three fierce cats. These he drove off with great difficulty, beating them back and bastooning them, where there were presently found three women of family and reputation so bruised and injured that they perforce kept their beds. All circumstances agreed beyond any shadow of doubt or incertitude. (*Malleus Maleficarum*, part ii, qn. i, ch. 9.) [49]

Next Bodin appeals to the authority of Pierre Mamor and Ulrich Molitor, a passage which will be found quoted in full below, and therefore need hardly detain us here.

He proceeds to remark that records of this shape-shifting are more commonly to be found in Greece and the East than generally in European countries, as witness the onslaught of werewolves into Constantinople, *anno* 1542, described by Job Fincel.

After a brief consideration of the word *Werwolf* or *loup-garou*, our author returns to his main theme and adduces the testimony of Pietro Pompanazzi, Paracelsus, Gaspar Peucer, Hubert Languet, Archbishop Olaf of Trondhjem, Abbot John Trithemius, and others, including at least one record by an eye-witness of werewolfism.

Next in order are surveyed the traditions and legends of antiquity, Homer, Herodotus, Pomponius Mela, Solinus, Strabo, Dionysius Afer, Varro, Vergil, Ovid, Pliny, and not a few writers more. For although it is freely allowed that the poets were merely reciting for our pleasure romantic fables, it is impossible to suppose that there was not some substratum of truth in a belief that was nothing less than universal both in place and time.

The traveller Pierre Belon [50] in his *Les observations de plusievrs singvlaritez et choses mémorables trouuées en Grèce, Asie, Indée, Egypte, Arabie et autres pays estranges*, Paris, 4to, 1553, relates that whilst at Cairo he saw a young itinerant juggler who possessed an ass which was able to do whatever his master bade him. The animal would, for example, go and kneel down before the fairest lady in the company if so ordered, and this be it noted he only did after he had cast his eyes round the circle, and he would also show that he was capable of such processes of ratiocination as are involved in a disjunctive hypothetical syllogism. It is strongly to be suspected that this ass was a man ensorcelled.

Bodin relates the incident told by Vincent of Beauvais,[51] and draws attention to the striking phrase used by S. Augustine concerning the recital made by Apuleius, " aut indicavit, aut finxit." [52] He also incidentally mentions the change of sex, as when girls seem to become boys, which cases in reality involve pseudohermaphroditic problems. (For these see F. L. von Neugebaber's *Hermaphroditismus beim Menschen* ; Krafft-Ebing, *Psychopathia Sexualis*, English translation by F. J. Rebman, 1906, pp. 352-364 ; Dr. Havelock Ellis, *Psychology of Sex*, vol. ii, *Sexual Inversion*, 3rd edition, 1927, pp. 315-16.)

Bodin stresses the point, which indeed is of first importance, that if lycanthropes " avoient poil et teste et corps " of the wolf, or in similar cases of the other animal, but " la raison ferme, et stable ", the sense of the Canon Episcopi is not in any way impugned. " Et par ce moyen la Lycanthropie ne seroit par contraire au canon Episcopi xxvi. q.v. ny à l'opinion des Theologiens qui tiennent pour la plurpart que Dieu non seulement a crée toutes choses, ains aussi que les malins esprits n'ont pas la puissance de changer la forme, attendu que la forme essentielle de l'homme ne change point, qui est la raison, ains seulement la figure." Which, theologically and philosophically is a perfectly sound proposition.

The authority of S. Thomas is accordingly cited, and Bodin glosses Isaias, xiii, 21, where it is said of the ruins of Babylon, " and the hairy ones shall dance there." This leads to a consideration of the magic sleights of Simon Magus before Nero, and more particularly of the metamorphosis of Nabuchodonosor to an ox with hairs like the feathers of eagles and nails like birds' claws.

As Nabuchodonosor was so punished by God, so Heaven may also well have permitted Gilles Garnier and the sorcerers of Savoy owing to their vile appetites and their lust for human flesh to have become wolves, losing human form.

From whatever cause this shape-shifting may arise, it is very certain by the common consent of all antiquity and all history, by the testimony of learned men, by experience and first-hand witness, that werewolfism which involves some change of form from man to animal is a very real and a very terrible thing. (It cannot, of course, take place without the exercise of black magic.) " Mais en quelque sorte que ce soit, il a pert que les hommes sont quelques fois transmuez en bestes demeurant la forme et raison humaine. Soit que cela se face par la puissance de Dieu immediatement, soit qu'il donne ceste puissance à Satan executeur de sa volonté."

Such briefly is the tenor of Bodin's famous chapter, and there is assuredly no impossible or unsound doctrine implicated in his theory as it stands, whatever falsity may have been, and indeed actually was, read into his thesis by his enemies.

The erudite Jean de Sponde in his *Commentary upon Homer*, folio, Basileæ, 1583, has a very ample note [53] upon the tenth book of the *Odyssey*, in which he discusses in detail the possibility of the transformation of the human shape to a beast, in reference to the magic of Circe. He says : " The general opinion is that the human frame cannot be metamorphosed into the animal bodies of beasts : but most hold that although there is no real shape-shifting the Devil can so cheat and deceive men's eyes that by his power they take one form, which they seem to see, to be quite another thing from what it actually is." From this he differs. The question is, whether men can be changed into animals, that is whether one body can be substantially transformed into another ? If one considers carefully and weighs the extraordinary and unknown forces of nature, or if one surveys the dark dominion of Satan, such a change is not to be deemed impossible. " I believe," he frankly admits, " that in the wide circuit of this world there are so many unknown and mysterious agents, that there may be some quality which effects this metamorphosis. I am very well aware that many of my readers will deem me impious or trivial." Jean de Sponde then advances the examples of the Arismaspi and Anthropophagi, and he speaks at length of noxious herbs, such as Cohobba, which grows in the isle of Haiti, and which drives men mad. Does not then this herb affect their reason ? Are not those possessed by the Devil wounded, as it were, in their souls ? And if a herb, and the power of evil, can have such control over the higher part of man, his reason and his immortal soul, why cannot a man's body be subject to similar disturbances ? The change, although corporeal and complete, may be considered accidental, not essential. We may well believe that the Devil will employ potions and unguents, having no power in themselves, to effect such metamorphosis.

The question is can men be turned into beasts ? " Possunt, inquam." *I affirm that they can be so changed.*

Jean de Sponde then refers to the authority of Bodin, " uiro eneditissimo & diligentissimo scriptore." He quotes various examples of werewolves, such as Gilles Garnier, Pierre Burgot, Michel Verdun, and others, cases which nobody would think of denying. That these foul warlocks were demoniac lycanthropes admits of no question, the point is how do we explain their lycanthropy.

It is sufficient for de Sponde to safeguard his position by acknowledging that a man cannot be said absolutely to be a wolf unless his soul change into the spirit of a wolf, and that is not possible. " Non posset ergo homo lupus fieri, nisi anima ipsa hominis, in lupi animam uerteretur omnino. Id autem fieri natura non patitur." He also adds : " Notandum est, nos non intelligere formam hominis in hac transfiguratione pensi : quia remanet eadem ratio, quae est uera forma, ex qua suum esse homo accipit." Which is the very position of Bodin, and cannot be said to be unorthodox, even if unusual.

Gaspar Peucer (1525–1602), the physician, son-in-law and friend of Melanchthon, in his *Commentarius De Praecipius Diuinationum Generibus*, 1553, "De Theomanteia," thus explains the shape-shifting of the demon werewolf : " Those who are changed suddenly fall to the ground as if seized with epilepsy, and there they lie without life or motion. Their actual bodies do not move from the spot where they have fallen, nor do their limbs turn to the hairy limbs of a wolf, but the soul or spirit by some fascination quits the inert body and enters the *spectrum* or φάσμα of a wolf, and when they have glutted their foul lupine lusts and cravings, by the Devil's power, the soul re-enters the former human body, whose members are then energized by the return of life." He holds it certain that the individual, the *ego*, becomes enclosed in a wolf's form, with bestial motions and ferocity.

Philippus Camerarius (1537–1624), the jurisconsult, some time Vice-Chancellor of the University of Altorf, in his *Operae Horarum Subcisiuarum Centuria Prima*, c. lxxii,[54] remarks that he has heard of werewolves from Gaspar Peucer and from Languet, but whether the metamorphosis is accomplished by some mysterious force of nature, or whether it is the effect of the divine wrath and a punishment as in the case of Nabuchodonosor he is unable to decide. With regard to the actual change of essential substance in the bodies he is by no means prepared to go so far as Bodin, with whom (he observes) some prudent and scrupulous writers do not entirely agree.

Jean Fernel, the physician of Henri II of France, in his weighty treatise *De Abditis Rerum Causis*,[55] lib. ii, cap. xvi : " Et Morbos, et Remedia quaedam trans naturam esse," certainly goes a very long way in support of Bodin. He mentions classical examples of metamorphosis, " de Demancho, quem narrat Plinius degustatis extis pueri immolati in sacrificio in lupum se conuertisse," and others ; adding, " Haec nisi multorum fide comprobata contestataque forent, non tam multas leges Iuris consultorum prudentia in magos tulisset." He amply allows for any glamour, since the demon not unseldom " solas rerum species et spectra quaedam exhibet, quibus hominum mentes quasi praestigiis illudat, et oculorum aciem praestringat."

In his very untrustworthy " Note on Witchcraft " given in the first volume (1886) of *Phantasms of the Living*, chapter iv,[56] Mr. Edmund Gurney says : " To be quite fair, I should add that Bodin says that one Pierre Mamor wrote a little tractate, in which he professed to have actually seen a transformation —this being the only case that I have come across where a man of sufficient education to write something that was printed is ever cited as bearing personal testimony to such marvels." The sneer is cheap and ignorant.

Bodin's actual words are as follows—I quote from the original edition, Paris, 4to, 1580, II, vi, p. 97—" Pierre Mamor en vn petit traicté qu'il a fait des Sorciers, dict auoir veu ce changement d'hommes en loups, luy estant en Sauoye. Et Henry de Coulongne au traicté qu'il a faict, *de Lamijs*, tient cela pour indubitable. Et Vlrich le Meusnier [57] en vn petit liure, qu'il a dedié à l'Empereur Sigismond, escript la dispute qui fut faicti deuant l'Empereur, & dit qu'il fut conclu pas viues raisons, & par l'experience d'infinis exemples, que telle transformation estoit veritable, & dict luy mesme auoir veu vn Lycanthrope à Constance, qui fut accusé, conueincu, condamné, & puis executé à mort apres sa confessiõ. Et se trouuẽt plusieurs liures publiez en Almaigne, que l'vn des plus grands Roys de la Chrestienté, qui est mort n'a pas long temps, souuẽt estoit mué en loup, & qui estoit en reputatiõ d'estre l'vn des plus grands Sorciers du monde."

It will be well, then, to see exactly what Mamor wrote, and to inquire who this " one Pierre Mamor " so scommatically referred to by Mr. Gurney was. Actually indeed he was a very distinguished scholar, whose attainments were held in highest esteem by his contemporaries.

Pierre Mamor was born at Limoges c. 1429–30. Upon 8th August, 1461, he was appointed rector of the Church of Saint Opportune at Poitiers at the instance of Bishop Louis Guerinet. It was about this time that the Bishop was translated to Frejus, but Pierre Mamor was equally honoured by Dom Jean du Bellay, O.S.B., who next wore the mitre of Poitiers. Mamor filled the Chair of Theology at Poitiers with such general applause that later he became the Rector of the University, a position he resigned upon being elected a Canon of the Cathedral of S. Peter at Saintes. His *Flagellum Maleficorum*, which was written 1461–70, and first printed at Lyons c. 1490, is appropriately dedicated to Louis de Roché-Chouart, who was Bishop of Saintes from 1460–1492.[58] It is obvious that the authority of so eminent a theologian as Canon Pierre Mamor must carry great weight and demands no small respect.

In his eighth and ninth chapters Mamor discusses at length the glamour and diabolical illusion, and shows that men are both objectively and subjectively deceived by the demon, their senses corrupted, cheated, and tricked ; the imagination clouded and betrayed. In chapter xi he treats of fascination and fantastical spells. The question of men who appear to be transformed into wolves or other animal forms arises. The classical legends of Circe and the wolves of Arcady are alluded to ; Apuleius is cited, the testimony of S. Augustine adduced. " De lupis uero quos ut dictum est berones siue galones uulgus uocat, uidetur esse dicendum, quod Daemon homines illos quos mutati in lupos asserunt, multi aliculi secreto retinent absconsos, et intrans corpus lupi alicuius, eum educit a siluis quem per uillas et agros discurrere cogit, et male plurima facit, occidit homines, pueros comedit, pecora deuorat et fugat, et plurimos homines terret." Nothing could be plainer. In Mamor's judgment the werewolf is a wolf possessed by the demon, who has cast the sorcerer into a deep trance meanwhile and concealed him in some secret spot. Mamor also points out how fearful and terrible a monster is the werewolf, a hell-possessed and devil-driven wolf, two fierce relentless enemies of man joined in one body of prey.

Our author then relates a werewolf story. A peasant's wife of Lorraine to her horror saw her husband vomit up a child's arm and hand, which he had devoured when he was in a wolf's form. " I believe," says Mamor, " that this was a demoniacal illusion." None the less, he adds, Pierre de Bressuire, a most learned and pious doctor, deemed that the human body could be metamorphosed to a lupine form corporeally, " but I prefer to go no further than S. Augustine, and I hold that when a werewolf rushed among the flocks and herds, tearing and ravaging, the body of the man was lying entranced in some secret chamber or retreat, whilst his spirit had entered and was energizing the form of a wolf."

Bodin, then, is hardly just in his adduction of Canon Mamor in full support of his especial view.

The *De Pythonicis Mulicribus* (1489), of Molitor, is cast in the form of a dialogue between Sigismund, Archduke of Austria ; Conrad Eschak, a chief magistrate of Constance ; and Ulrich Molitor, who was a Professor of Pavia. In caput iii they argue whether the form of a man may be changed. Sigismund says, No, and quotes the Canon Episcopi. Conrad mentions the crafts of Simon Magus, who so altered the face of Faustinianus that all thought this latter to be the wizard himself. Ulrich argues that men can be metamorphosed into wolves and other animal shapes by the power of the demon, who does not in truth create anything new but only makes something seem to be which actually is not. A proposition denied by nobody. The same points are taken up in caput viii, and Molitor definitely speaks of glamour, " Dæmones perstringendo oculos faciant apparentiam, qua homo iudicat rem alterius formae esse, quam sit, ita ut quis uidens hominem, credat eum esse asinum uel lupum et temen unusquisque retineat formam suam, quanquam oculi nostri decipiantur et ad aliam speciem erroneo iudicio deducantur."

It is not to be denied that in the case of the demoniac werewolf there is a change, both subjective and objective, so that the warlock seems to be a wolf both to himself and also is seen as a wolf by all who observe him.

It must be sufficient to cite only a few of the very many

eminent authorities who discuss the actuality of the metamorphosis of man to a bestial shape.

Although the tractate *De Spiritu et Anima* is certainly
not to be assigned to S. Augustine, this work has so often
been quoted as by the great doctor that it will not be amiss
in passing to cite the famous passage thence to which appeal is
found again and again in older writers. " It is very generally
believed that by certain witches' spells and the power of the
Devil men may be changed into wolves and beasts of burthen,
and as pack-animals be made to bear and carry loads, and
when their work is done they return to their original shapes,
but they do not lose their human reason and understanding,
nor are their minds made the intelligence of a mere beast.
Now this must be understood in this way, namely that the
Devil creates no new nature, but that he is able to make
something appear to be which in reality is not. For by no
spell nor evil power can the mind, nay, not even the body
corporeally, be changed into the material limbs and features
of any animal . . . but a man is fantastically and by illusion
metamorphosed into an animal, albeit he to himself seems
to be a quadruped, and as for the burthens which the beast
carries if they be real they are supported and borne by
familiars so that all who see the seeming animal may be
mocked and deluded by diabolical glamour." [59] But, as we
have pointed out, the work is spurious and as such carries
no especial weight.

A more important passage is chapter xviii of the Eighteenth
Book of the *De Ciuitate Dei*, whose rubric runs : *Of the
deuills power in transforming mans shape : what a Christian
may beleeue herein.* (I quote the English version of John
Healey, folio, 1610.) [60] In chapter xvii, S. Augustine has
treated *Of the incredible changes of men that* Varro *beleeued,*
namely, the strange tales of that famous witch and excellent
herbarist Circe, the metamorphosis into wolves of the
Arcadians ; nor does Varro "thinke that *Pan* and *Iupiter*
were called *Lycæi* in the Arcadian history for any other
reason then for their transforming of men into wolues : for
this they held impossible to any but a diuine power : a wolfe
is called λύκος in greeke, and hence came their name *Lycæus* ".

What then are we to hold touching this deceit of devils ?
In principio, " the greater power wee behold in the deceiuer,

the firmer hold must we lay vpon our mediator." It is ludicrous and trivial to make a sweeping assertion and say airily that all these legends are lies. " For when I was in Italy," writes the holy doctor, " I heard such a report there, how certaine women of one place there, would but giue one a little drug in cheese, and presently hee became an asse, and so they made him carry their necessaries whither they would, and hauing done, they reformed his figure againe : yet had he his humane reason still, as *Apuleius* had in his asse-ship, as himselfe writeth in his booke of the golden asse ; bee it a lie or a truth that hee writeth (*aut indicauit aut finxit*). Well either these things are false, or incredible, because vnusuall. But we must firmely hold Gods power to bee omnipotent in all things : but the deuills can doe nothing beyond the power of their nature (which is angelicall, although maleuolent) vnlesse hee whose iudgements are euer secret, but neuer vniust, permit them. Nor can the deuills create any thing (what euer shewes of theirs produce these doubts), but onely cast a changed shape ouer that which God hath made, altering onely in shew. Nor doe I thinke the deuill can forme any soule or body into bestiall or brutish members, and essences : but they haue an vnspeakable way of trans-porting mans fantasie in a bodily shape (*phantasticum hominis*) vnto other senses (this running ordinarylie in our dreams through a thousand seuerall things, and though it be not corporall, yet seemes to cary it selfe in corporall formes through all these things) while the bodies of the men thus affected lie in another place, being aliue, but yet in an extasie farre more deepe then any sleepe. Now this phantasie may appeare vnto others sences in a bodily shape, and a man may seeme to himselfe to bee such a one as hee often thinketh himselfe to be in his dreame, and to beare burdens, which if they be true burdens indeed, the deuills beare them, to delude mens eyes with the apparance of true burdens, and false shapes. For one *Praestantius* told me that his father tooke that drug in cheese at his owne house, wherevpon he lay in such a sleepe that no man could awake him : and after a few daies hee awaked of himselfe and told all hee had suffered in his dreames in the meane while, how hee had beene turned into an horse and carried the souldiours victualls about in a budget. Which was true as he told, yet seemed it but a dreame vnto him. . . . So then those Arcadians, whom the god (nay the deuills rather) turned into wolues, and those fellowes of *Vlisses* beeing charmed by *Circe* into Bestiall shapes, had onely their fantasie, occupied in such formes, if there were any such matter. But for *Diomedes* birds, seeing there is a generation of them, I hold them not to be transformed men, but that the men were taken away, and they brought in their places, as the hinde was in *Iphegenias* roome, *Agamemnons* daughter. The deuill can play such iugling trickes with ease, by Gods permission, but the Virgin beeing found aliue afterwards, this was a plaine deceipt of theirs to take away her, and set the hinde there. But *Diomedes* fellowes, because they were neuer seene (the euill angells destroying them) were beleeued to bee turned into those birds that were brought out of their vnknowne habitations into their places."

Very important in this connection, the power of the Devil to effect the transformation of men into animals, is the tenor of the Canon Episcopi.[61]   This Canon is first met with in the collection of ecclesiastical decrees, *De ecclesiasticis disciplinis*, ascribed to Abbot Regino of Prüm, A.D. 906. Actually it is certainly much older than the period of Regino himself, and even if it be considered as a genuine piece of legislation enacted by some Council, this was assuredly not the Synod of Ancyra, A.D. 314, to which it is generally ascribed as " Ex concilio Anquirensi ".   In any case this Canon 371 passed into the Collections of Ivo of Chartres and Gratian.

The rubric runs : " De mulicribus, quae cum daemonibus se dicunt nocturnis horis equitare."   In the first part are denounced and condemned " certain wicked women who turning aside to follow Satan, and being seduced by the illusions and phantasms of demons, fully believe and openly profess that in the dead of night they ride upon certain beasts with the pagan goddess Diana [or with Herodias] and a countless horde of women, and that in these silent hours they fly over vast tracts of country and obey her as their mistress, while on other nights they are summoned to pay her homage ".

John of Salisbury speaks of this popular belief in a witch-queen named Herodias,[62] whilst Lorenzo Anania [63] has

THE TRANSVECTION OF WITCHES

" A maribus pariter ac feminis nonnullis crebro hunc nefandum actum exerceri legimus hunc *Dianæ* ac *Herodiadis* ludum uulgo appellant ". There are many similar allusions, and from these Girolamo Tartarotti in his *Del Congresso Notturno delle Lamie*, published at Rovereto in 1749, evolved the extraordinary idea that witchcraft was a remnant or a continuation of a pagan cult he was pleased to dub the *Società Dianiana*,[64] a foolish maggot taken over (without acknowledgement) and re-presented with singular ill-success in a more modern work, wherein is proclaimed as a wondrous new discovery " this ancient religion the Dianic cult ".

Leaving fantasy and fable it must be remarked that the Canon Episcopi is not at all concerned with witchcraft but with pagan creeds and practice. The transvection of witches by demoniacal agency is a thing amply assured, but their evil flights to the Sabbat are quite another thing from the aerial coursing through the skies led by ethnic goddesses whom they worship and adore.

The point is aptly discussed by Francisco Vittoria, in his *Relectiones undecim*,[65] Salamanca, 1565, *De arte Magica*, where whilst duly insisting upon the transvection of witches by diabolical agency, a thing proved by authority, by the experience of eye-witnesses, and by their own free confession, says that it is false and impossible that they should ride with Diana and Herodias. " Nam Diana nulla est, Herodias autem est in inferno, nec permittitur exire ei, nec est mulier, sed sola anima."

The clause in the Canon which immediately concerns us is the conclusion : " Whosoever therefore believes that any-thing can be done in this way, or that any creature can be changed for better or for worse or transformed into another species or kind save by God the Creator Himself, Who hath made all things and by Whom all things were made, of a certainty he errs in a matter of faith [and is worse than a very heathen]." This last phrase is very ambiguous, and was bound to cause perplexity and fallacies not a few.

The Dominican Nicolas Jaquerius in his *Flagellum Haereti-corum*,[66] cap. ix, " De Consideratione caute habenda circa illud c. Episcopi," very sharply snibs those who misreading the import of the Canon on this account hinder and impede the prosecution of sorcerers, and so in a real sense become fautors of this horrid craft. He shows that the authority of the Canon Episcopi is indeed very slight, and it is most awkwardly worded since as it stands it appears clean contrary to Scripture. He concludes in reference to the last clause : " Qui igitur credit, quod modo praedicto ministerio Daemonum, res aliquae possint de nouo immutari, aut etiam de nouo aliqua corpora formari, hic fidem non perdit, quin potius rectam et catholicam fidem tenet, quicquid dicatur in saepe dicto allegato c. Episcopi."

It were easy, but I think superfluous, to run through a number of writers who have glossed this final clause and set it in its right interpretation. One may well stand for many more. Pierre Mamor in the seventeenth chapter of his *Flagellum Maleficorum* well explains the meaning of the Canon which has been so persistently misunderstood. To resume : There can be no question here of the transvection of witches. That is proved, and approved by immense authority. This clause is directed against those who superstitiously believe that Diana or Herodias are in any sort goddesses possessed of divine or supernatural power, which is assuredly an ethnic creed.

When it is laid down by the Canon that any who hold a creature may be changed not immediately by divine power but by divine permission are in error. We can only say that this clause is awkwardly and badly worded, since S. Paul tells us that Satan can transform himself into an angel of light : " haec omnia informiter et crude dicta sunt, et contra hoc quod prius dictum est, quod sathanas transfigurat se in Angelum lucis." [67]

S. John Chrysostom in his Twenty Eighth (Twenty Ninth) *Homily on S. Matthew*, says that a demon may feign and simulate to be the ghost of one departed. But this is all illusion. The demon cannot essentially change one being to another, no, neither a disembodied nor a corporeal being. He cannot essentially change the body of a man into the body of an ass : καὶ οὔκ ἄν τις ἀνθρώπου σῶμα ὄνου (σῶμα) ἐργάσαιτο. [68]

S. Thomas, *Summa*, pars 1, qu. cxiv, 4 art., says that God alone can work real miracles, but the demons are permitted to perform lying wonders, extraordinary to us, and they employ certain seeds that exist in the elements of the world by which operation they seem to effect transformations. The Devil can from the air compose a body of any form or shape and appear in it ; so he can clothe any corporeal thing with any corporeal form to appear therein.

The Seraphic Doctor, S. Bonaventura, in his *Commentarium in Secundum Librum Sententiarum*, Dist. vii, p. 11, art. 11, Quaest. 11,[69] teaches us that demons can by their own power produce artificial forms, but natural forms they cannot produce of their own power, but only by some other force or power. The demon produces forms or changes shapes by some natural force which he knows how to employ, fashioning to his will the secret elemental seeds of things. The same Saint, in Distinctionem viii, *De potestate daemonum respectu hominum*, p. 11, Art. Unicus, Quaest. iii,[70] decides that evil spirits may mock and cheat our senses in three ways : (1) by exhibiting as present what is not really there ; (2) by exhibiting what is there as other than it really is ; (3) by concealing what really is there so that it appears as if it were not.

Alexander of Hales in his *Summa*,[71] Pars secunda, qu. xliii, treats " De praestigiis et miraculis magorum ", and in the First Article of Membrum i discusses those miracles of sorcerers wrought " secundum delusionem et phantasiam ". He concludes that the demon can make things appear other than they really are, a delusion which is subjective as well as objective. This is other than a mere sleight, which is not objective. The delusion may be wrought " per se et per accidens. Et per se dupliciter : proprium et commune ".

In his *Quaestio de Strigibus* [72] Fra Bartolomeo Spina devotes the eighth chapter to a consideration whether witches by diabolical art can turn men and women into brute beasts. He writes that although the demon cannot make material new forms, which is essentially an act of Creation, he can so confuse, commingle, and intermix already existing forms that fantastically he represents to any who behold the human form in a brute shape. Nay more, the subject of such diabolical art and working will steadfastly believe that he is become such or such an animal, and will act according to that brute nature.

So King Nabuchodonosor " was cast away from among men, and as an oxe did he eate grasse, and with the dew of heauen his bodie was imbrued : til his heares grew into the similitude of eagles, & his nailes as it were of birds ".[73]

" It is no matter for wonder that when certain women are deluded and deceived by diabolic and fantastical agencies they exhibit the very nature, the form and likeness, the agility and feline proclivities of cats, and they are persuaded that they are cats, whilst those of their company believe them to be cats, and they in turn believe that those of their society are also cats. This is amply proven by the free confessions of such women."

An explanation of this may very well be that the demon has from certain natural elements formed an aerial body in the shape of a cat, and interposing this fantastical body between the sight of the eyes and the essential human body he thus deceives and deludes one and all.

No thinking person can deny that these witches in the form of cats suck the blood of children and overlook them, and indeed not unseldom kill them by diabolical agency. That many such delusions are wrought cannot be doubted, and the supernatural method in which this is accomplished may be ambiguous. It may be admitted that witches are themselves often mocked and tricked by the demon when they think they are actually cats, and even when they deem they are sucking the blood of some child, for as the demon impresses upon their imagination and vision the form of some animal so may he offer to their sight and taste some fluid of the colour and savour of blood. For as S. Thomas allows, the Devil can entirely bemuse and cheat the senses.

At the same time it is very probable, and indeed it has often been known to happen, that witches do actually and indeed suck children's blood, which they draw either by some sharp needle or by the scratch of their long nails, or else by the aid of the Devil they pierce some vital vein, and scars are left in the tenderest parts of the child's body, whence they have sucked the hot life-blood, and the child becomes anaemic, wastes away, and dies. This cannot be gainsaid since it is proven by irrefragable testimony, and it has been demonstrated that after witches in the form of cats have been seen to attack children, blood is noticed to trickle and trill from wounds, although they may be very small, and accordingly the Devil hath been busy there.

That these cat-witches should find their way most stealthily and silkily into bedchambers, leap walls, run with exceeding nimbleness and speed, and in every way behave as grimalkins wont, is not at all surprising, for they accomplish these actions by the Devil's aid, who assists them lending them excessive fleetness, a swift motion impossible to natural man. Many who have seen these cat-witches have borne witness to these facts, and such circumstances are amply proven and received.

In fine, I doubt whether the whole matter has better been summed up than here. For as the Devil aids the cat-witch, this demon animal that has all the proclivities of a cat, so will he energize the werewolf, who will thus be possessed of all the savagery and fiercest instincts of a ravening wolf.

Sprenger and Kramer, the authors of that great and admirable book, the *Malleus Maleficarum*, therein devote question x of part i to the inquiry *Whether Witches can by some Glamour Change Men into Beasts*.[74] They review the Canon Episcopi and certain arguments of S. Thomas, which must be rightly understood. They then reach the conclusion that "the devil can deceive the human fancy so that a man really seems to be an animal", with a reference to S. Antoninus, *Summa*, pars i, tit. ii, c. vi.[75] Examples are given, such as will be shown in later chapters. The Canon is more nearly examined, and it appears that " when it says that no creature can be made by the power of the devil, this is manifestly true if Made is understood to mean Created. But if the word Made is taken to refer to natural production, it is certain that devils can make some imperfect creatures ". S. Albert the Great, in his book *On Animals*,[76] says that devils can really make animals, that is to say, "they can, with God's permission, make imperfect animals." Upon this I would remark that many—but not all—authorities hold that the werewolf has no tail. Whence, if such be the case, it is clear the Devil can make a werewolf. The *Malleus* proceeds to debate several points already treated, and therefore not necessary to set out in detail here.[77]

The great demonologists, Remy, Guazzo, and Boguet,[78] have all discussed the problems of werewolfery at length and with much learning, but as their works are easily accessible it were almost superfluous to repeat their arguments here, the more especially since Remy and Guazzo are agreed that metamorphosis, true in appearance but not in essential fact, is caused by the glamour wrought by the demon. Shape-shifting has the form but not the reality of that which it presents to the sight. Boguet very wisely says : " There is much disputing as to whether it is possible for men to be changed into beasts, some affirming the possibility, whilst others deny it, and *there are ample grounds for both views*."

It may not be impertinent to remark that the erudite Abbot John Trithemius, when relating a case of werewolfism in his *Chronicon Hirsaugiense*,[79] of Baianus, Prince of Bulgaria, a most cunning magician who could transform himself into animal shape, says that we cannot doubt the metamorphosis was accomplished by black magic and the Devil's aid, but actually how it took place we do not know, and it is best not to inquire over curiously therein.

Certain writers, none certainly of the first, nor perhaps yet of the second, order, incline towards a sceptical view of lycanthropy. Thus Martin Biermann, in his *De Magicis Actionibus*,[80] 1590, written directly to controvert the view of Bodin, is unwilling to allow much more than that the Devil can stir up depraved appetites and drive men to imagine themselves in some wild frenzy brute beasts. If men do appear as wolves it must be explained as some objective glamour.

Johann Georg Godelmann has as rubric of the third chapter of book ii of his *De magis, ueneficis, et lamiis*, 1591, *De Lamiarum et aliorum hominum in Lupos, feles, aliaue eiusce-modi animantia transformatione*. He argues against a real and actual metamorphosis, although he admits that demons appear as wolves, attack and slay men. Generally speaking, the shape-shifting must be held to be " praestigiosam et phantasticam ".

Wilhelm Adolph Schreiber, of Marburg, in his *De physiologia Sagarum*,[81] gives it as his opinion that witches cannot materially change into cats, dogs, hares, and other animals ; nor can they transform others by their spells. " Apparens ista et phantastica omnis fuit uisio, fucataque, et umbratilis tantum imago, ut homines quidem maneant, sed brutorum animantium specie extrinsecus apparantes solummodo uideantur. Imago scilicet uel ab ipso Cacodæmone, eiusue auxilio, uel ex mera illorum, quos hoc modo mutatos esse dicimus, imaginatione orta. Facilimum enim est dæmone Sagarum corpora alterius cuiusdam bestiæ siue rei cuiuslibet figura aut imagine superinducta tegere, ne quales sint homines agnoscentur."

The Minim Pierre Nodé, in his *Declamation contre l'Erreur Execrable des Maleficiers Sorciers, Enchanteurs, Magiciens, Deuins, & semblables obseruateurs des superstitions,*[82] only touches on lycanthropy in passing, and paraphrases S. Thomas with allusions to S. Augustine and the Canon Episcopi.

Bishop Binsfeld, in his learned *De Confessionibus Maleficorum,*[83] points out that the Devil cannot work true miracles, and hence he denies that witches and enchanters can by their evil power essentially change them to wolves, cats, or any other animal ; there is no *transmutatio totius in totum.* The metamorphosis then is *secundum apparentiam.*

In his *De Spirituum Apparitionibus,*[84] Peter Thyraeus, S.J., sometime Professor of Theology at Trèves, Mayence, and Würzburg, gives very ample consideration to lycanthropy, to which indeed he devotes chapters fifteen to twenty-five of his Second Book.

Since he covers—although, be it remarked, with a learning and clarity that rank him with the foremost—much the same ground as other writers with whom we have already dealt in ample detail—whilst paying fit tribute to his erudition, the elegance of his style and vigour of exposition, it is hardly necessary to do more than take a comparatively brief survey of this important piece. He first marshals the various instances of metamorphosis from legend, from tradition, from history, from contemporary records and trials. Upon these he builds a thesis which is seemingly so firm and logical as not to be traversed and rebutted. He does not spare to emphasize the cogency of these arguments, the force of these examples, and he expressly says : " We must not venture too rashly to accuse and reprehend those authors who have deemed that a shape-shifting to the form of wolves, asses, or cats may be actual and real." Yet he proceeds to search out the flaw in his former indagation, so carefully and so nicely planned, and after much subtle philosophical inquiry and theological argument he not without difficulty arrives at the conclusion that a man cannot be transformed by another nor transform himself essentially and absolutely into the body of a beast.

When it is asked how is this metamorphosis then effected, Thyraeus sums up various opinions. Some hold that this shape-shifting results from mere hallucination. This may be waived, as it certainly will not hold good in the vast majority of cases. Others consider that the form of an animal is superimposed in some way upon the human form. Others again believe that persons are cast in a deep slumber or trance by the demon's power, and that then the astral body is clothed with an animal form.

Thyraeus favours an explanation on the lines that by the power and agency of the fiend both the man himself and all who espy him are fully persuaded and convinced that he is metamorphosed to the shape of some animal, wolf, cat, or another, what it may be, whereas actually he is not so transformed. For the demon, be it observed, can energize with superhuman agility, gigantic strength, and a tenuous pliancy almost amounting to volatility the bodies of demoniacs and the possessed.

It is disappointing to find that the genius of Martin Delrio, in his masterpiece, *Disquisitionum Magicarum Libri Sex*,[85] deals with werewolfism in a somewhat summary and condensed chapter. It is not improbable, of course, that he intended to handle so difficult a subject in a separate treatise. Be that as it may, Delrio in his Second Book, Quaestio xviii, inquires : *An corpora ex una in aliam speciem Magi queant transformare ?* He had already mentioned the subject in his notes upon Seneca's Tragedies, *In L. Annæi Senecæ . . . Tragœdias decem*, Antwerp, Plantin, 4to, 1576 ; *Agamemnon*, v. 690, and he at once refers to S. Augustine and the Canon Episcopi. This latter he stresses, as I venture to think, unduly. To the disease lycanthropia he gives a few lines, directing us for details to the physicians. He then relates a history from Bartolomeo Spina and an instance of werewolfism at Dixmude which came under his own notice, as will be detailed later. He refers to the case of Peter Stump, and also draws attention to Binsfeld, Remy, Lorenzo Anania, and Claude Prieur's *Dialogue*. Delrio would offer as his explanation of werewolfism a fantastical body formed by the demon from the elements and obtruded or superimposed upon the lycanthrope, which he supposes to have happened in the case of Gilles Garnier of Dôle. I may be wrong, but in reading Delrio upon lycanthropy I cannot divest myself of the impression that he has given us a meagre selection from his notes upon this subject; and, as I suggest above, I conceive that in view of a fuller dissertation he refrained from but touching upon it somewhat superficially here.

Pierre le Loyer in his *Discours et Histoires des Spectres, Visions, et Apparitions des Esprits,*[86] Livre ii, ch. 7, writes *de la transmutation des Sorciers et sorcieres.* His explanation of any metamorphosis of witches attributes shape-shifting to diabolical glamour, the demon imposing a lupine or feline form upon his slave. Le Loyer, who snibs Bodin at every turn, seems to misunderstand that great writer very grossly, and his unwonted animus betrays him into some errors which go far to vitiate this section, the weakest undoubtedly in his whole vast work.

Dr. Tobias Tandler, who held the Chair of Mathematics at Wittenberg at the beginning of the sixteenth century, in his *Dissertatio de Fascino,* a public disputation held in the University on 24th October, 1606, and printed that same year,[87] busied himself in controverting propositions nobody ever thought of maintaining in regard to animal transformations, and finally involved himself in a muss of words, misconceptions, and inexactitudes.

Strozzi Cicogna, in his *Pelagio degli Incanti,* Vincenza, 1605, translated into Latin by Gaspar Ens as *Magiae Omnifariae Theatrum,* Coloniae, 1606, part i, lib. iv, cap. 5,[88] has a very ample treatment of the question *An daemones corpora hominum in alias species transformare, ac sexum mutare queant?* He posits at the outset that neither by the utmost power of the demon nor by any natural force can the body of a man be organically changed into the animal species. For God created the various species of living things, as we are told in the first chapter of Genesis, and the handiwork of God cannot be altered. (That is to say, it cannot be essentially altered. For it might be argued that the body of Job was altered when by the Devil's action it was covered with a loathly ulcer, as God permitted.)

With regard to reincarnation Cicogna has much to say, and he is at some pains to disprove these theories, but his arguments hardly concern us directly here. Nor need we feel ourselves detained in this place by the example of Nabuchodonosor, and it will suffice to note that our author considers a species of madness to have fallen upon the King of Babylon, who had incurred the wrath of God, and therefore he wandered forth lunatic into the fields living as a wild animal, but in no way transformed to a beast.

The disease of lycanthropy is next dealt with, after which Cicogna reviews at some length the various well-known instances of shape-shifting and werewolfism. These, as he remarks, being reported by solid authors cannot be disputed or denied. He regards, then, werewolves as demon-wolves, not the witch in that shape, but a devil who assumed the form of a wolf. The witch meanwhile is held in an evil trance, what time the Devil impresses on the imagination of the sleeper those acts of destruction he himself has accomplished in lupine shape.

A curious dissertation upon changes effected in sex concludes this chapter. Many examples are proferred, and he rather fantastically adds : " Neroni quidem in emasculando atque in feminam transformando Sporo conatus irritus fuit. Idem quum Heliogabalus conuocatis medicis in se ipso tentasset, ut Uenerem utramque experiretur, sic ab eis tractus fuit, ut nec mas amplius nec femina esset, dignam scilicet tam turpi ac diabolico conatu mercedem consequutus."

It were barely possible to review all the particular tracts concerning lycanthropy which were written throughout the sixteenth and seventeenth centuries, and indeed so prolonged a task were superfluous since of necessity we find a certain repetition both in the expository and in the arguments, whilst from the multiplicity of varied examples the most important (if not all) will be given in their due place in later chapters here. A couple of examples then may suffice for all.

The *Dialogue de la Lycanthropie ou Transformation d'Hommes en Loups vulgairement dits Loups-garou et si telle se peut faire*, written in 1595 by an observant Franciscan of the Louvain house, Frère Claude Prieur, was published early in 1596,[89] " Chez Iehan Maes, et Philippe Zangre," at Louvain. The work was examined and approved by Heinrich de Cuyek, Bishop of Ruremonde, whilom Chancellor of the

Theological Faculty of Louvain, and Gilles Cheheré, Professor of Theology at Louvain, as also by Frère Gerard Jacé, the provincial, and Frère Arnold Ysch, the Guardian of the Louvain house, so it comes from the Press with full weight of authority. After a lengthy preface the *Dialogue*, wherein the interlocutors are Eleion, Scipion, and Proteron, commences on p. 13 B and occupies 120 well-filled pages.

The " forme of a Dialogue " was no doubt adopted "*for to make this treatise the more pleasaunt and facill*", as King James once wrote of his own *Dœmonologie*.

The speakers commence by bewailing the misfortunes of their time, whilst they acknowledge the justice of divine chastisement. Never, they cry, did Satan rage up and down more furiously. Men in their wickedness have become worse than the very beasts of the field and are as ravening wolves. Hence the question, poised by Eleion, easily arises, can a man actually shift his shape and transform himself into a wolf ? Scipion and Eleion maintain that such a corporeal and essential metamorphosis is possible, and Proteron (who stands for the author) proceeds to enlighten them. It is hardly needful to follow him through all his intricate theological and philosophical debate, in the course of which he takes occasion to controvert many Platonic and Pythagorean ideas, in particular the theory of reincarnation. The true sense of Our Lord's words concerning the Baptist : he is Elias that is to come, S. Matthew, xi, 14, is insisted upon and expounded. There had been some suggestion, it appears, bruited among the vulgar that the souls of men returned and were reincarnated in wolves.

Proteron, or Claude Prieur, declares that wolves are the natural agents of God's wrath, and he tells how in the year 1587, when he was preaching in Perigord and for several months was living in a little Minorite convent at Rions, about five leagues from Bordeaux, it so happened that on S. John's day, 27th December, he was sent by the Guardian to say Mass at a remote village some little way distant. On his return, passing near a hamlet, he met a poor woman all in tears, who told him that only half an hour before a huge wolf had snatched up a little girl who was playing at the door of her hut, and in spite of all that she or her neighbours could do the child was carried off into the forest.

The Guardian, Père de Roca, informed Claude Prieur that the ravages of wolves in that district had reached such a height that men could only go to work armed and together in numbers.

Some three or four years later, when Prieur was stationed at Rodes, the cloisters one night about ten o'clock rang and re-echoed with most horrible howling. The whole company were greatly alarmed as the sound had an unearthly note. The porter of the convent, all trembling, informed the religious that he had seen in the pale moonlight a pack of eighteen or twenty wolves who swept resistlessly through the streets at hurricane speed. Their teeth gleamed sharp and white ; their red tongues hung from their hot panting jaws ; their eyes glinted horribly ; and the grey fur bristled as they ran. It seemed as though it were a hunt of demons who passed in headlong course.

Prieur remarks that after All Saints Day the villagers expect wolves to invade the very houses, coming down in packs from the mountains of Auvergne, driven by hunger from their lair. The good father himself met a wolf in the environs of Villefranche, and only drove off the animal with great difficulty.

It is hardly to be doubted that the Devil often possesses the bodies of wolves and drives them to madness, then urging and lancing this furious host against men.

A very great many examples are debated of cannibalism, of sorcerers who rifle cemeteries and cook young children. Amongst others Gilles de Rais is mentioned. There are also the lycanthropes, who have been brought to trial and executed for this crime, Pierre Burgout, Michel Verdun ; those of whom Olaus Magnus tells ; the cases related by Peucer ; Peter Stump of Bebur, near Cologne, and very many more. How can one explain this mass of evidence ? " Il ne semble plus qu'on puisse doubter," says Scipion.

However, Proteron commences to examine the proposition at considerable length according to the scholastic method, and with references to S. Augustine, S. Thomas, S. Bonaventura, Richard Petrus de Aquila, Dionysius the Carthusian, Durandus, Alexander of Hales, Bartolomeo Spina, Binsfeld, Petrus Thyraeus, Alfonso a Castro, and other doctors, he demonstrates that according to these authorities there cannot be a corporeal transformation, whether wrought by an enchanted girdle or unguents or by any means whatsoever. None the less, lycanthropy is a fact not to be denied. Where then shall we seek an explanation ? What do we see when we espy a werewolf ? Sometimes we behold a real body, not created indeed but newly formed from existing elements by Satan ; sometimes it is a fantastical shape.

There next arises the question of King Nabuchodonosor,[90] and the glosses of the great Biblical exegetes are passed in review.

The virtue of the Sign of the Cross is lauded, and Prieur has a very striking pronouncement : " L'heresie et magic sont fort parens, depuis que tout Magicien est heretique."

The hideous abuse of the Most Holy Sacrament by sorcerers is spoken of, and the prevalence of necromancy deplored. God is praised in the deliverance from possession of Nicole Aubry, a celebrated case, who was deluded by a demon feigning to be the shade of her grandfather, but at last unmasked as Beelzebub.[91]

After an eloquent peroration the treatise concludes with six resolutions : (1) Animals and brute beasts are sometimes made the instruments of Heaven's wrath ; hence (2) wolves may be energized by unusual savagery in their mission, or they may be veritably possessed by demons ; (8) there are not lacking examples of men, some of whom were sorcerers, and some who perchance were not, that have given themselves over to cannibalism ; (4) an essential transformation, the which involves creation, is not according to Catholic teaching, since neither unguents, nor haunted streams, nor incantations, nor magic girdle, nor Satan himself can effect such transformation. Wherefore lycanthropy must be explained in some other way as has been duly expounded. (5) Sorcerers by diabolical aid, or demons, can assume some other shape or form, and this appears to be real, both subjectively and objectively, but is in the strictest and narrow sense fantastical. (6) Let us use the methods Holy Church has provided, the Sign of the Cross, the Rosary, Sacramentals, and other pious practices to arm ourselves against the Devil, who if we are so fortified cannot harm or hurt us. Above all, let us frequently sign ourselves with the healthful and life-giving Sign of Salvation which dispels all enchantments, and as Jacob with his staff only passed

over Jordan, so let us by the Cross pass through this world
to everlasting felicity and eternal glory. Amen.

A gentleman of Angers, Sieur de Beauvoys de Chauvincourt,
in his *Discours de la lycanthropie ou de la transmutation des
hommes en loups*, Paris, 1599, after a review of the various
histories of werewolves, both ancient and more recent cases,
concludes that the fittest explanation lies in the power of the
Devil who by his craft produces a glamour that is both
subjective and objective, deceiving both the sorcerer and
those who behold him. This change is wrought by means
of unguents, powders, potions, and noxious herbs, which
are able to dazzle all who come under their baleful and magic
effluence. This opuscule is slight and, I venture to think,
adds little to the solution of these dark and vexed problems.

A direct and particular answer to Bodin, *De la Lycanthropie,
Transformation, et Extase des Sorciers*, by Sieur Jean de
Nynauld, Docteur en Medecine, was written in 1614, and
published at Paris in the summer of the following year.[92]
A tractate of 109 pages, it was approved, 6th April, 1615,
by two Doctors of the Sorbonne, Colin and Forgemont, as
being orthodox and containing no proposition contrary to
the Catholic Faith. It is dedicated to the Primate of France,
Cardinal Jacques du Perron, Archbishop of Sens.

The work is divided into seven chapters, the several rubrics
of which will serve adequately to show its scope. Chapter i,
*That the Devil cannot in any way transform men into beasts.
Moreover, the Devil cannot separate the soul of a sorcerer from
the body, in such fashion that after a while the soul returns to
the body and the sorcerer is alive.* It would not require much
to qualify these propositions as heretical. The first posit
is clearly contrary to S. Augustine's teaching, which we have
shown. Chapter ii, *Of the Simples which enter into the composition of the witch's ointment, and what particular virtue each has.*
Nynauld lists : " la racin de la belladonna, morelle furieuse,
sang de chauue sourris, d'huppe, l'Aconit, la berle, la morelle
endormante, l'ache, la saye, le pentaphilon, l'acorum vulgaire,
le persil, fueilles du peuplier, l'opium, l'hyoscyame, cyguë,
les especes de pauot, l'hyuroye, le *Synochytides*, qui fait
voir les ombres des Enfers, c.d., les mauuais esprits, comme
au contraire, *l'Anachitides* faict apparoit les images des
saincts Anges."

Chapter iii, *Of the Composition and use of the first Ointment which Sorcerers confect.* Chapter iv, *Of the Composition and use of the second Ointment which Sorcerers confect.* Chapter v, *Of the Composition and use of the third Ointment which Sorcerers confect.* In the course of this last chapter Nynauld remarks : "Regarding the reality of this metamorphosis of men into beasts I have already proved that it cannot be achieved by any natural means, nor even by the Devil even if he strain to the utmost of his power, for he cannot even make a fly. God alone is the Creator and Preserver of all things." There is flat heresy here. It is a solemn truth which nobody would think of denying to say that God alone can create. In the eighth chapter of Exodus it is written that "Aaron stretched forth his hand upon the waters of Ægypt, and the frogges came up, and covered the Land of Ægypt. And the enchanters also by the enchantments did in like manner, and they brought forth frogges upon the Land of Ægypt ".[98] It was the power of Satan by God's permission which brought forth these frogs. Therefore Nynauld plainly contradicts the sense of Scripture.

Chapter vi, *Of Lycanthropy*, the disease.

Chapter vii, *Of those natural things which have the quality of presenting to the imagination things which are not present in reality but only in effect.* Such for example are strong potions, and drugs as hasheesh, strychnos, and preparations of belladonna. The vapour and incense of violent perfumes will also dazzle and cheat the senses. Nynauld concludes that all shape-shifting is mere hallucination, and he ends up this chapter with a fling at miracles, which he declares to look for to-day would be a sign of infidelity and weak faith. Here he plainly shows the cloven hoof, and one can only remark that it is surprising such a passage should have been permitted by the censors.

As an Epilogue he adds a *Refutation of the Opinions and Arguments which Bodin sets forth in the Sixth Chapter of his Demonomania to attest the reality of Lycanthropy.* This is a piece without value, and only remarkable for the fact that when he has contradicted Scripture and the Fathers, denied tradition and experience, in a fine roulade at the end Nynauld congratulates himself upon having vindicated the Bible, the Doctors and Fathers of the Church, the Theologians and Philosophers, nay even the very Pagans and ethnic writers themselves.

I have designedly left until this point a consideration of the *Oratio pro Lycanthropia* of the learned and judicious Wolfeshusius, a celebrated Professor of Leipzig. This was delivered at Leipzig on the 4th of February, 1591, and printed at that town, quarto, shortly after in the same year. Wolfeshusius poises the question : Fierine queat, ut homo per Magiam seu Daemonis artem lupi aut alterius bestiae formam uerè assumat induatque, aut an omnia λυκομανία illa, quae de gente potissimum Arctoa scriptis autorum memoratur phantasticè sit et ex iudicii Dei prauatione existat. " Is it possible that a man may by magic spells or the power and craft of the Devil verily and indeed assume, and transform himself into the shape of a wolf or some other animal, or are all those histories and accounts which we read of lycanthropy in particular as detailed in authors who have written of the peoples of far Northern climes, merely fantastical, and if we accept them do we in any way seem to impugn the omnipotence of Almighty God ? " The mention of the Arctic writers seems especially to refer to Olaus Magnus.

Wolfeshusius in the course of an erudite and acutely argued disquisition sums up various theories which have been advanced to explain lycanthropy. Some hold it is " morbum ex praua humorum corporis dispositione ortum uel merum diaboli hominis salua corporis figura demendantis praestigium ", that is to say a disease, or maybe a diabolic hallucination. Others again prefer to think that " per Satanae praestigiis glaucoma quasi quoddam animo hominis per ·fascinatos inter et extra sensus obiciatur, quò feram aliquam bestiam se esse credat, eiusque mores imitando exprimet ", that the Devil casts both a subjective and objective glamour upon the werewolf, who not only believes himself to be a very wolf and acts as such, but also when seen by others is taken to be a fierce howling wolf.

Yet a third explanation is that the Devil casts the sorcerer into a trance, " stuporem arte diabolica immissum in lupos aliqui se falsè credant transformatos." The evil one " mirifica somnia excitet iisque confudat imaginibus ", whilst the actual witch is drenched and overtaken with sleep, " corpora collapsa atque sopita."

Some endeavour to sustain a trivial argument : " friuolam alteram de Lycanthropia opinionem qui solum illusione quadam Satanae aspicientium oculos perstringi aiunt." Werewolfism resolves itself into a mere jugglery : the Devil cheats the eyes of those who see the werewolf.

Wolfeshusius refers to the following lines from Book IV, *Aprilis*, of the *Fasti*,[94] a well-known poem by Blessed Baptista Mantuan, the Carmelite, who speaking of various perils says :—

> Adde lupos, qui tartareis agitantibus ambris
> In furias acti, ne dum iumenta per agros,
> Audebant laniare homines, et in urbibus ipsis,
> Casibus hic perculsi omnes diuina coacti
> Quærere subsidia, et Diuos excire precando.

These occur in the *De Litanea Minore*, ll. 13–17, a description of the gang-days.

After citing two or three more authors, Wolfeshusius sums up by saying that " uiri undequaque celebres et docti " support Bodin in his explanation of lycanthropy, and concludes : " conati sumus efficere ut ueritas patefieret mirandae illius immutationis, qua hominum Magica ac diabolica arte in brutum uerti posse, tum ueterum saeculis creditum esse, tum hoc tempore communi rumore peruulgatum."

It is incidentally worth noting that he has a reference to the transvections by the black art of Faust : " Et patrum aetate Faustus, qui pallio securi insidentem ad longinquas terras baiulasse fertur."

It will here be interesting to consider one or two of the more modern views of lycanthropy. Adolphe d'Assier, in his *Posthumous Humanity* [95]—I quote from the English translation made by Henry S. Olcote and expressly sanctioned by the author of the *Essai sur l'Humanité Posthume et le Spiritisme, par un Positiviste*—chapter xi, writes : " I will finish this study of the mesmeric personality with some views upon lycanthropy. This feature, perhaps the most obscure of the manifestations of the fluidic being, long seemed to me so utterly unreasonable that I did as with questions of posthumous vampire and the incubus—I turned over without reading the pages that treated of this theme, and I gave but a very inattentive hearing to what was told me about these singular metamorphoses. If I decide to speak of it now, it is because it would not be wise to oppose a systematic denial to a multitude of facts reputed authentic which corroborate each other."

Two recent and very striking cases of werewolfism are then related, and d'Assier sums up with the utmost frankness, a candour which wins our respect and which we should be glad to see more widely imitated. He writes : " I shall not attempt to give an explanation of these prodigies, which are, in fact, an insoluble problem for myself. The fluidic and, consequently, elastic nature of the mesmeric personality permits of its adapting itself to lycanthropic forms ; but where shall we place the efficient cause of these meta-morphoses ? Must we fall back upon atavism ; in other words, upon the most delicate and least-known chapter of biology ? I prefer to confess my incompetency, and to leave to those who are more skilled than myself the task of expounding the enigma."

In *The Mysteries of Magic* [96] Éliphas Lévi writes : " We must here speak of lycanthropy, or the nocturnal transforma-tion of men into wolves, histories so well substantiated that sceptical science has had recourse to furious manias, and to masquerading as animals for explanations. But such hypotheses are puerile, and explain nothing."

This author gives it as his opinion that werewolfery is due to the " sidereal body, which is the mediator between the soul and the material organism ", and largely influenced by a man's habitual thought being attached by strong sympathetic links to the heart and brain. Thus in the case of a man whose instinct is savage and sanguinary, his phantom will wander abroad in lupine form, whilst he sleeps painfully at home, dreaming he is a veritable wolf. The body being subject to nervous and magnetic influences will receive the blows and cuts dealt at the fantastical shape.

C. W. Leadbeater, in his *The Astral Plane, its Scenery, Inhabitants and Phenomena*, [97] offers a theosophical explana-tion of the many problems concerning vampires and were-wolves. His view is that certain astral entities are able to materialize the " astral body " of a perfectly brutal and cruel man who has gained some knowledge of magic, and these fiends drive on this " astral body ", which they mould into " the form of some wild animal, usually the wolf ", to blood and maraud.

In his monograph, *The Book of Were-Wolves*,[98] Baring-Gould is inclined to attribute werewolfery, the terrible truth of which he does not for a moment evade, to a species of madness, during the accesses of which the person afflicted believes himself to be a wild beast and acts like a wild beast. " In some cases this madness amounts apparently to positive possession."

Mr. Elliott O'Donnell, in his *Werwolves*,[99] remarks that " the actual process of the metamorphosis savours of the superphysical ". The werewolf is sometimes in outward form a wolf, sometimes partly wolf and partly human. This may be the result of the fact that he is " a hybrid of the material and immaterial ". The opinions of those whose views of the werewolf postulate a complete denial of the supernatural need not, I think, detain us here, and are in themselves unworthy of record.[100]

We may now proceed to inquire how this change, the shape-shifting, was effected. In the case of those who were metamorphosed involuntarily, the transformation was, of course, caused by some spell cast over them through the malignant power of a witch.[101]

With regard to the voluntary werewolf, under whom for this consideration we may include any kind of shape-shifting. In the first place, an essential circumstance and condition is a pact, formal or tacit, with the demon. Such metamorphosis can only be wrought by black magic. This is in itself a mortal sin, for, as S. Bonaventura instructs us (*In II Sent.*, Dist. vii, p. 11, art. ii, quaest. iii),[102] it is sinful to seek either counsel or aid from the demon. Again, the werewolf is a sorcerer well versed and of long continuance in the Devil's service, no mere journeyman of evil. For Guazzo tells us [103] : " this seems particularly worth noting : that just as Emperors reserve certain rewards for their veteran soldiers only, so the demon grants this power of changing themselves into different shapes, as the witches believe, only to those who have proved their loyalty by many years of faithful service in witchcraft ; and this is as it were a reward for their long service and loyalty. This was amply proved by Henry Carmut in the year 1588 by his own particular confession, coming after that of many others of his sort."

In the first place, the sorcerer strips himself mother-naked. In certain obscure magical rites nudity was required. The witch of whom Giovanni Battista Porta speaks [104] cast aside all her clothes before she smeared her limbs with fatty grease as a preparation for her journey to the sabbat. The Four Witches, as portrayed by Dürer, are naked for the sabbat orgy, as also are the witches in the celebrated pictures by Hans Baldung, who depicts the confection of the witches' salve, the anointing of the brooms, and the horrid crew in full flight to their Satanic synagogue. Jaspar Isaac, in his *L'Abomination des Sorciers*, portrays these abandoned ministers and slaves of the demon divesting themselves of their garments in hot haste to repair to a nocturnal rendezvous. Equally elaborate is the detail in Frans Francken's *An Assembly of Witches*, where the women are undressing for their dark revels, and one naked witch is already being anointed. A woodcut in Keisersberg's *Die Emeis*, ed. 1516, 36^b, depicts three naked *unholden* raising a storm. Teniers and Queverdo, in their several pictures *Le Départ pour le Sabat*, have drawn nude witches at the moment they commence their diabolic transvection, whilst Goya's *La Transformation des Sorciers* shows us four hideous naked warlocks, one of whom, already metamorphosed to a wolf, is about to take his flight by the chimney, through whose yawning aperture is fast disappearing yet another of the foul fraternity. It will be remembered that the soldier in Petronius divested himself of his clothes before the lupine metamorphosis.[105] In one of the most famous of the were-wolf trials, that of Pierre Bourgot and Michel Verdun in December, 1521, by Frère Jean Boin, O.P., Prior of the house of Poligny and General Inquisitor for the diocese of Besançon, Pierre Bourgot confessed that in order to effect the shape-shifting into a wolf's form, he cast off his clothes and anointed his naked body with the mysterious salve. Michel Verdun was changed into a wolf whilst he was yet clad, which is noted by Weyer [106] as altogether exceptional.

The unguent used by the werewolf was, according to Weyer, that employed by witches in their transvection. De Lancre justly sees in this unction a mockery of the Holy Chrism at Baptism : " Satan est le singe de Dieu : il void qu'au Baptesme les Chrestiens sont oincts du sainct Chresme comme athletes, pour entrer au combat contre les vices et Esprits immondes . . . Le Diable graisse les siens et mesme les loups-garoux comme ses athletes en tous ses malefices." [107] Ulisse Aldrovandi, in his *De Quadrupedibus Digitatis Uiuiparis*, observes : " olei . . . Lupi sunt amantissimi." [108] There are constant references to the use of this ointment by the demoniac lycanthropes. As we have just seen, it was employed by Pierre Bourgot and Michel Verdun. Guazzo in the first chapter of his Second Book says : " The ointment they use is either given them by the demon or brewed by themselves with devilish art." [109] Boguet in his forty-seventh chapter speaks of lycanthropes rubbing themselves with the ointment before the metamorphosis. In his twenty-fourth chapter he even more precisely says, when treating of their unguent : " The witches anoint themselves with it when they go to the Sabbat, or when they change into wolves." [110] De Lancre notes that the werewolf Jean Grenier, who was tried in 1603, smeared himself with this liniment of hell : " Il rapporte auoir esté graislé et parle du pot de graisse que le malin Esprit luy gardoit." [111] Delrio in the second book, *Disquisitionum Magicarum*, quaestio xviii, speaks of certain anointings and spells the werewolf employs : " ad hoc inunctionibus certis (ut Dolani ille Lycanthropi, de quibus Acta iudicaria sunt edita) uel solis uerbis utuntur." [112] Elich, in his *Daemonomagia*, quaestio xii, repeats this when treating of werewolves : " inunctionibus certis . . . uel solis uerbis conceptis utuntur." [113] Claude Prieur, also, in his *Lycan-thropie*, draws attention to the baleful unguent of the werewolf, and De Lancre in his *Tableau de l'Inconstance des Demons*, livre iv, discours 4,[114] notes how the Demon impresses a lupine shape on the sorcerers " quand les loups-garoux se sont graissez de certaine graisse ".

It will readily be remembered that Vergil, in the Eighth Eclogue, the *Pharmaceutria*, has a reference to these witch ointments, lines 96–100, a passage which Dryden turns thus :—[115]

> These poys'nous Plants, for Magick use design'd,
> (The noblest and the best of all the baneful Kind),
> Old Mœris brought me from the Pontick Strand ;
> And cull'd the Mischief of a bounteous Land.
> Smear'd with these pow'rful Juices, on the Plain,
> He howls a Wolf among the hungry Train :

And oft the mighty Negromancer boasts,
With these to call from Tombs the stalking Ghosts :
And from the roots to tear the standing Corn ;
Which, whirld aloft, to distant Fields is born.

In his *De Miraculis Rerum Naturalium Libri IIII*,
Antverpiae, Ex Officina Christophori Plantini, 1560, lib. ii,
cap. xxvi,[116] Giovanni Battista Porta has a section *Lamiarum
unguenta*, which is as follows : " Quae quanquam ipsae
superstitionis plurimum admiscent, naturali tamen ui euenire
patet intuenti ; quaeque ab eis acceperim referam. Puerorum
pinguedinem ahaeno uase decoquendo ex aqua capiunt,
inspissando quod ex elixatione ultimum, nouissimumque
subsidet, inde condunt, continuoque inseruiunt usui : cum
hac immiscent eleoselinum, aconitum, frondes populneas, et
fuliginem. Uel *aliter* sic : Sium, acorum uulgare, pentaphyllon, uespertilionis sanguinem, solanum somniferum, et
oleum, et si diuersa commiscent, ab iis non parum dissidebunt,
simul conficiunt, partes omnes perungunt, eas antea per-
fricando, ut rubescant, et reuocetur calor, rarumque fiat,
quod erat frigore concretum : Ut relaxetur caro, aperiantur
pori, adipem adiungunt, uel oleum ipsius uicem subiens, ut
succorum uis intro descendat, et fiat potior uegetiorque :
id esse in causam non dubium reor. Sic non illuni nocte per
aera deferri uidentur, conuiuia, sonos, tripudia, et formosorum
iuuenum concubitus, quos maxime exoptant : tanta est
imaginationis uis, impressionum habitus, ut fere cerebri pars
ea, quae memoratiua dicitur, huiusmodi sit plena : cumque
ualde sint ipsae ad credendum naturae pronitate faciles, sic
impressiones capessunt, ut spiritus immutentur, nil noctu
diuque aliud cogitantes, et ad hoc adiuuantur, cum non
uescantur nisi betis, radicibus, castaneis, et leguminibus.
Dum haec pensiculatius perquirendo operam nauarem :
ancipiti enim immorabar iudicio, incidit mihi in manus
uetula quaedam, quas a strigis auis nocturnae similitudine
striges uocant, quaeque noctu puerulorum sanguinem e
cunis absorbent, sponte pollicita breuis mihi temporis spatio
allaturam responsa : iubet omnes foras egredi, qui mecum
erant acciti testes, spoliis nudata tota se unguento quodam
ualde perfricuit, nobis e portae rimulis conspicua : sic
soperiferorum ui succorum cecidit, profundoque occubuit
somno, foris ipsi patefacimus, multum uapulat, tantaque uis

soporis fuit, ut sensum eriperet, ad locum foras redimus, iam medelae uires fatiscunt, flaccescuntque, a somno seuocata, multa incipit fari deliria, se maria, montesque transmeasse, falsaque depromens responsa, negamus, instat, liuorem ostendimus, pertinaciter resistit magis. Sed quid de eis sentiam ? dabitur alias narrandi locus, ad institutum nostra redeat oratio : satis enim prolixiusculi fuimus. Hoc praeterea praemonendum censeo, ne facile experientes dilabantur, non haec aeque omnibus euentura : sed inter caeteros melancholicis, cum natura praealgida, algiosaque sint, eorumque uaporatis multa non sit : recte enim quae uident percipiunt, et referre possunt."

In 1562 was printed at Cologne, 12°, *Magiae Naturalis, siue de Miraculis Rerum Naturalium Libri IIII*, and the above passage duly appears, II, xxvii, pp. 197 and 198.

However, in the edition *Io. Bapt. Portae Neapolitani Magiae Naturalis Libri XX*, " ab ipso authore expurgati," Naples, folio, 1589, which was approved and licensed by the Dominican Fra Tommaso de Capua, 9th August, 1588, this passage is not included. Indeed, the work has been most thoroughly revised, and the four books of the original are now divided into twenty, with additional matter, excisions, and variations. The only cognate passage seems to be in the second chapter of the eighth book, *De Medicis Experimentis*, pp. 150–2, *Of Physical Experiments*. (I quote from the English translation of Porta, *Natural Magick in XX Bookes*,[117] London, folio, 1658.) In the preface Porta complains : " *A certain Frenchman in his Book called* Daemonomania, *Tearms me a Magician, a Conjurer, and thinks this Book of mine, long since Printed, worthy to be burnt,*[118] *because I have written the Fairies Oyntment, which I set forth onely in detestation of the frauds of Divels and Witches ; That which comes by Nature is abused by their superstition, which I borrowed from the Books of the most commendable Divines. . . . I pass over other men of the same temper, who affirm that I am a Witch and a Conjurer, whereas I never writ here nor elsewhere, what is not contain'd within the bounds of Nature.*"

Nevertheless Porta merely mentions *Medicines which cause sleep.* He describes *How to make men mad with Mandrake* ; and how " To make a man believe he was changed into a Bird or Beast ", which is done by infusing mandrake, stramonium or solanum manicum, belladonna, and henbane, into a cup of wine. Porta says that he has known those who on drinking this menstruum imagined themselves to be fish, endeavouring to swim ; or geese, hissing and trying to peck grass, and similar idle fancies. " These, and many other most pleasant things, the curious Enquirer may finde out : it is enough for me only to have hinted at the manner of doing them."

Weyer gives the condiment of these unguents in his *De Lamiis*, iii, 17,[119] exactly following, and indeed reproducing Porta's own phrase. The first liniment, then, is composed of the fat of young children seethed in a brazen vessel until it becomes thick and slab, and then scummed. With this are mixed *eleoselinum*, hemlock ; *aconitum*, aconite ; *frondes populeae*, poplar leaves ; and *fuligo*, soot.

The second formula is : *sium*, cowbane ; *acorum uulgare*, sweet flag ; *pentaphyllon*, cinquefoil ; *uespertilioris sanguis*, bat's blood ; *solanum somniferum*, deadly nightshade ; and *oleum*, oil.

In the eighteenth book, " De Mirabilibus " of his *De Subtilitate*,[120] Girolamo Cardano gives a recipe for the confection of the witch-ointment. He mentions the lamiae, " quae apio, castaneis, fabis, cepis, caulibus, phaselisque uictitantes, uidentur per somnum ferri in diuersas regiones, atque ibi diuersis modis affici, prout uniuscuiusque fuerit temperies. Iuuantur ergo ad haec unguento, quo se totas perungunt. Constat ut creditur puerorum pinguedine e sepulchris eruta, succisque apii aconitique tum pentaphylli siligineque. Incredibile dictu quanta sibi uidere persuadeant : modo laeta, theatra, uiridaria, piscationes, uestes, ornatus, saltationes, formosos iuuenes, concubitusque eius generis quales maxime optant : reges quoque et magistratus cum satellitibus, gloriamque omnem et pompam humani generis, multaque alia praeclara, uelut in somniis et picturis quae maiora sunt quam quae natura praestare possit. Uelut et contraria ratione tristia, coruos, carceres, solitudinem, tormenta. Neque id mirum, quanquam ueneficum, ad naturales enim causas traduci debet."

Cardano goes on to describe various unguents, which (he says) not only induce sleep but cause dreams of certain kinds, glad or sorry. He mentions that he has himself made trial of " uulgatum unguentum quod Populeon a frondibus populi dicitur ".

Here then we have for the witch-ointment, the fat of children, whose bodies have been dug from the grave ; henbane ; aconite and cinquefoil. I presume the fine wheaten flour was added to make a thick paste.

Dr. Jean de Nynauld discusses the composition of these unguents in his *Les ruses et tromperies du Diable descouvertes*, Paris, 1611, and again in his *De la Lycanthropie*, 1615, where the rubric of the second chapter runs : " Des Simples qui entrent en la Composition des Onguents des Sorciers & de leur vertu en generale." Chapters three to five enlarge upon the uses of these witches' ointments.

Dr. J. B. Holzinger, who, however, does not mention Nynauld, has devoted a detailed monograph to the subject, *Zur Naturgeschichte der Hexen*, Graz, 1883.

Dr. H. J. Norman informs me that these witches' concoctions could of themselves have no effect.

The spells recited by the sorcerer about to shift his shape to a werewolf are profane and horrible in the last degree. To inquire into these were impious ; they were accursed to know. Unfortunately some such mantras have been preserved in ancient grimoires and evangels of Satan, which I will not specify too nearly. As Boguet [121] tells us, witches can indeed cause injury by mere words and uttered spells, for barbaric jingle and meaningless though the phrases be, they are none the less a potent and energetic symbol of the pact between the witch and Satan. Yet, be it remarked, the sounds and syllables have not of themselves, when spoken by another, the power to hurt and kill, neither has the mere spell (as Leonard Vair and Bodin also write) [122] a malign quality of itself to shift the human shape into bestial form.

Merely as a piece of folk-lore, interesting and sufficiently curious, there can be no harm in giving here the *zagovór* " to be employed by a wizard who desires to turn into a werewolf ", as supplied by W. R. S. Ralston in his *Songs of the Russian People* [123] : " In the ocean sea, on the island Buyán, in the open plain, shines the moon upon an aspen stump, into the green wood, into the spreading vale. Around the stump goes a shaggy wolf ; under his teeth are all the horned cattle ; but into the wood the wolf goes not, into the vale the wolf does not roam. Moon, moon! golden horns! Melt the bullet, blunt the knife, rot the cudgel, strike fear into man, beast, and reptile, so that they may not seize the grey wolf, nor tear from him his warm hide. My word is firm, firmer than sleep or the strength of heroes."

Ralston comments: " In this spell, says Buslaef (*Istor. Ocherki*, i, 86), the aspen stump is mentioned because a buried werewolf or vampire has to be pierced with an aspen stake. The expression that the wolf has all the horned cattle in or under his teeth resembles the proverb now applied to St. George, ' What the wolf has in his teeth, that Yugory gave '—St. George, or Yegory the Brave, having taken the place which was once filled by the heathen god of flocks, the Old Slavonic Volos. And the warm hide of the werewolf is in keeping with his designation *Volkodlak*, from *dlaka*, a shaggy fell."

Peter Thyraeus, S.J., *De Spirituum Apparitionibus*, liber ii, cap. xxxiv, 326, speaks of these metamorphoses being seemingly accomplished by " unctiones corporibus adhibitas, incantationes et carmina, baptismata, siue in aquas immersiones, caseum, uel alium aliquem cibum, poculum denique certis uerbis incantatum ".[124]

Olaus Magnus, *A Compendious History of the Goths, Swedes, and Vandals*,[125] book xviii, chapter 82, *Of the Fiercenesse of men who by Charms are turned into Wolves*, writes: " The reason of this metamorphosis, that is exceeding contrary to nature, is given by one skilled in this witchcraft, by drinking to one in a cup of Ale, and by mumbling certain words at the same time, so that he who is to be admitted into that unlawful Society do accept it. (Liber xviii, cap. xlvi: per poculum ceruisiae propinando, dummodo is, qui huic illicito consortio applicatur, illud acceptat, certis uerbis adhibitis consequitur.) Then when he pleaseth he may change his humane form, into the form of a Wolf entirely, going into some private Cellar, or secret Wood. Again, he can after some time put off the same shape he took upon him, and resume the form he had before at his pleasure." Here then a ritual draught was drunk whilst the spell was muttered o'er by unhallowed and fearful lips.

The transformation was sometimes effected by donning a girdle made of the pelt of the animal whose shape was to be assumed, or else made of human skin, which must be that of a murderer or some criminal gibbeted or broken on the wheel for his offences. The girth was three fingers wide. It will be borne in mind that formerly the girdle was an essential part of a man's attire. Again, the demon presented the sorcerer with such a girdle in hideous mockery of the Cincture of S. Augustine, the Black Leather Belt of S. Monica, S. Augustine, and S. Nicolas of Tolentino. This Belt, which forms a distinctive feature of the habit of Augustinian Eremites, originated in a vision of S. Monica, who received a black leather belt from Our Lady. Such a belt is worn by members of the Archconfraternity of Our Lady of Consolation.[126] Guazzo particularly informs us that the witch upon her solemn profession of witchcraft is required to cast away this holy girdle should she be wont to wear it.[127]

Peter Stump, who was condemned for werewolfism in 1590, confessed that the demon has bestowed a girdle upon him, with which he girt himself when the lust came upon him to shift his shape to a wolf. Elich calls particular attention to this, and speaks of the Succubus who gave the wizard lycanthrope this belt : " ille ab hac donatus fuerat zona, qua cum cingebatur, et sibi et aliis in lupum uerti credebatur." [128]   Claude Prieur also notes that Stump possessed " une telle ceinture laquelle auoit telle force que de la transmuer et lycanthropier quand bon luy sembloit ".[129] Delrio, also, does not forget to mention Stump, executed only some ten years before, " eo quod cum dæmone succuba plus quatuor lustris consuesset ; ab hac donatus fuit lata quadam Zona, qua cum cingebatur, et sibi et aliis in lupum uerti uidebatur." [130]

It will be remembered in this connection that Richard Rowlands—from whom there has been occasion to quote before—in his *Restitution of Decayed Intelligence*, 1605, wrote how the " *were-wolves* are certaine sorcerers, who hauing annoynted their bodyes, with an oyntment which they make by the instinct of the deuil ; and putting on a certain inchanted girdel, do not only vnto the view of others seeme as wolues, but to their own thinking haue both the shape and the nature of wolues, so long as they weare the said girdel. And they do dispose theselues as uery wolues, in wurrying and killing, and moste of humaine creatures " [131]

The wolf-girdle passed into common tradition, and was in the opinion of the vulgar perhaps the most usual way (after the magical ointment) of shape-shifting.

Sometimes the demon assigned a complete hide or wolf-skin to the sorcerer, as is duly noted by Delrio : " Aliquando uero hominibus ipsis ferarum exuuias huiusmodi ueras aptissime circumdat : quod fit quando illis dat lupinam pellem in trunco quopiam cauae arboris occulendam, ut ex quorundam confessionibus constat." [132] Elich closely follows this : " dat [dæmon] pellem lupinam in trunco quodam cauae arboris occultandum, ut ex quorumdam confessionibus in confesso fuit." [133]

The werewolf Jean Grenier [134] told De Lancre of his wolf's skin. " Ce ieune garçon m'accorda qu'il auoit vne peau que Monsieur De la forest luy auoit donnee en la forest de Droilha, qui est près la parroisse de sainct Anthoine de Pison, dans le Marquisat de Fronsac, laquelle il cachoit sur le toict d'vne grange en son païs, non pas qu'il la luy portast toutes les fois qu'il le vouloit faire courir." He also confessed that " ce Mõsieur (le demon) se trouua deuant luy, et luy bailla aussi tost vne robbe de peau de loup qu'il vestit, puis en forme de loup il se jetta sur le plus petit des trois enfans ".

Boguet, that great and erudite judge, tells us that during the trials of the lycanthropes, " The confessions of Jacques Bocquet, Françoise Secretain, Clauda Jamguillaume, Clauda Jamprost, Thievenne Paget, Pierre Gandillon, and George Gandillon are very relevant to our argument ; for they said that, in order to turn themselves into wolves, they first rubbed themselves with an ointment, and then Satan clothed them in a wolf's skin which completely covered them, and that they then went on all-fours and ran about the country chasing now a person and now an animal according to the guidance of their appetites." [135]

We must remind ourselves that, under God's permission, all these transformations are wrought by diabolic power.

A werewolf of whom Gervase of Tilbury speaks assumed the form of a wolf by rolling naked for a long while in the sand.[136]

Other methods of transformation, such as the drinking of water out of the footprint of a savage wolf ; eating the brains or flesh of the animal ; drinking from haunted streams or pools ; plucking and wearing, or smelling to the lycanthropic flower ; the chawing of some herb ; however interesting, and indeed significant, in themselves, all seem to belong to the domain of folk-lore, and hardly concern us here.[137]

It may be remarked, however, that Pliny, in his *Natural History*, liber viii, cap. 36,[138] says that the Spaniards believe there is a certain poison in a bear's head, and if this be distilled and a man drink thereof he will imagine himself a bear. This is noted by Weyer,[139] who says that he knew of a certain Spanish grandee who having eaten of bruin's brain rushed forth out of the city to the lonely hills and deserts, prowling up and down, and imagining that he had been transformed into a bear.

It may now be asked how the removal of the shape was effected and the return to the human form duly accomplished. By divesting himself of the wolf's skin or the girdle the sorcerer was able to recover his man's body, and the glamour dispersed. The lycanthropes whom Bodin tried said " that when they wished to resume their former shape, they rolled in the dew or washed themselves with water ".[140] This agrees with Sprenger's statement that a man who has been changed into a beast loses that shape when he is bathed in running water.[141] Again, the man mentioned by Vincent of Beauvais, who was changed into an ass, resumed his human shape when he was dipped in the water.[142]

Gervase of Tilbury writes that according to many authorities the werewolf recovers his shape if he be maimed and a member be lopped off his lupine body.[143]

In some parts of France, as for example la Creuse, it is believed that those who wander in the skin of the loup-garou are suffering souls, and that the wolf thanks the man who is brave enough to withstand and wound him, thus securing his deliverance. " Chaque nuit, ils sont forcés d'aller chercher la maudite peau à un endroit convenu et ils courent ainsi jusqu'à ce qu'ils rencontrent une âme charitable et courageuse qui les délivre en les blessant." [144] " Lous loups-garous soun gens coumo nous autes ; mès an heyt un countrat dab lou diable, e cado sé soun fourçatz de se cambia en bestios per ana au sabbat e courre touto la neyt. Ya per aco un mouyén de lous goari. Lous cau tira sang pendent qu'an perdut la forme de l'home, e asta leu la reprengon per toutjour." [145]

That there is some truth at any rate in these relations seems certain, and thus they have been preserved in French tradition. A writer of Périgord tells how at the beginning of the nineteenth century it was believed in this district that at each full moon certain lads, particularly the sons of priests, are compelled to become werewolves. They go forth at night when the impulse is upon them, strip off their clothes and plunge naked into a certain pool. As they emerge they find a number of wolf-pelts, furnished by the demon, which they don and thus scour the countryside. Before dawn they return to the same pool, cast off their skins, and plunge into the water again, whence emerging in human form they make their way home.[146]

The werewolves of the Montagne Noire at the beginning and end of their metamorphosis also dived deep into certain pools.[147]

At Guéret (la Creuse) a haunted stream called **La Piquerelle** was long reputed to be the spot where the wizard werewolf lurked waiting for his prey. The foul beast would suddenly leap out on passers-by, but if the stranger wounded him so that his blood flowed, he fled howling.[148]

Exorcism and, above all, the Blessed Sacrament of the Altar will disperse all glamour and objectively restore to human shape those upon whom an evil spell of fascination and metamorphosis has been cast. In which connection the history related by the authors of the *Malleus Maleficarum* [149] is very memorable, and must not be omitted here.

The events took place in the city of Salamis about the year 1450, or a little earlier. A trading-vessel having put in at that port there went on shore one of the company a likely enough young man, who during his view of the town came to a little house on the sea-shore at the door of which was standing a woman. He asked her if she had any eggs to sell, and the woman after some delay brought out some eggs, bidding him haste back to his ship ere it set sail. When the young merchant arrived at the vessel, which was still hulling and showed no signs of weighing anchor, being hungry he determined to eat the eggs, and presently he found himself dumb, without the power of speech. Amazed and sick at heart he wished to go on board, but the mariners drove him off with sticks, bawling out : " Look what this ass is doing !

Curse the beast, you are not coming on board." When he persisted they redoubled their blows, and he was obliged to take to flight. Wandering sadly hither and thither he found that everyone saw and regarded him as a donkey, and at length he took his way to the woman's house to beg relief. This witch, however, kept him for three years, compelling him as a beast of burden to carry loads and serve her businesses. His only consolation was that although everybody else took him for an ass, the witches themselves, severally and in company, who frequented the house, recognized him as a man and he could talk to them in human accents. At length in the fourth year the youth was driven to the city by the woman, and it chanced she followed some way behind. Passing by a church, the door of which was open, he heard the sacring-bell ring at Holy Mass—for it was the Latin rite—and he saw the Body of the Lord lifted up by the priest. Whereupon he kneeled in the street, bending his hind legs, and lifting his forelegs, his hands, over his head in adoration of his God. It so happened that some Genoese merchants observed this, and swiftly came the witch to belabour the ass with her stick. The merchants, however, seized her, and caused both her and the ass to be taken before a judge, where presently she confessed her crimes and was compelled to restore the young man to his proper form. He then returned, giving thanks to God, to his own country, and the evil woman paid the penalty her sorceries most justly deserved.

We may well believe, and indeed are very well assured, that by this signal instance of God's mercy, devotion to the Blessed Sacrament was wonderfully increased in those parts.

Here then we have a notable example of diabolical glamour dissolved by the might of the Blessed Sacrament.

Such ensorcellments may also be put an end to by exorcism, for as S. Cyprian says in his Letter to Magnus, " by the power of the exorcist whose words are energized in the sovranty of Almighty God the Devil is exceedingly chastised, yea, and burned as with fire and sore tormented." [150] Again, in his *Liber Apologeticus*, addressed to Demetrianus, proconsul of Africa, the same Saint writes : " If you could but hear and see how what time the possessed and demoniacs are exorcized and smitten, as it were, with spiritual blows, the demons screeching and yowling, are compelled to abandon the bodies they have so foully invaded, and release the afflicted from their travail and pain." [151]   Some very ancient forms of exorcism, traditionally ascribed to S. Basil the Great and doubtless written or used by that father, may be found in Migne, *Patres Graeci*, vol. xxxi (1678–1684).   In Migne, *Patres Latini*, vol. lxxxvii (929–954), are given some very valuable *Formulae Ueteres Exorcismorum et Excommunicationum*,[152] of which number x is clearly applicable to werewolfism.

To the domain of folk-lore of a very ancient tradition would seem to belong such beliefs as that which tells us the shape of the werewolf will be removed if he be reproached by name as a werewolf, or if again he be thrice addressed by his Christian name, or struck three blows on the forehead with a knife, or that three drops of blood should be drawn. That he should be saluted with the Sign of the Cross is, of course, natural to any Christian.   Some say that the werewolf may recover his human form by shifting the buckle of his strap (*úlf-heðnar*) to the ninth hole.[153]

It may be asked if a person who has the fearful power of shape-shifting can be in any way recognized.   It is almost certain that a mysterious and unnatural horror must lower about these bond-slaves of Satan, and the animal will devour the human as when their ears become pointed and they lope stealthily in their walk.   Boguet notes that the werewolves who came before him to be tried, owing to their nocturnal coursings through briars and brambles over the countryside, " were all scratched on the face and hands and legs ; and that Pierre Gandillon was so much disfigured in this way that he bore hardly any resemblance to a man, and struck with horror those who looked at him." [154]

De Lancre describes the werewolves as follows :   " Ceux qui ont figure de loups comme ce ieune garçon ont les yeux affreux et estincelans comme loups, font les rauages & cruautez des loups, estranglent chiens, couppent la gorge auec les dents aux ieunes enfans, prennent goust à la chair humaine comme les loups :

Eadem feritatis imago
Colligit os rabiem et fuso iam sanguine gaudet :[155]

ont l'addresse et resolution à la face des hommes d'executer tels actes, leur dents et leur ongles sont fortes et aigusees cōme celles des loups, ils trouuent goust à la chair crue comme loups, ils courent à quatre pates, et quand ils courent ensemble ils ont accoustumé de departir de leur chasse les vns aux autres, et s'ils sont saouls ils heurlent pour appeller les autres : s'il n'en vient point ils enseuelissent ce qu'il leur reste pour le garder : dans Albert le Grand li. 22. *De animali.*"

When De Lancre visited the werewolf Jean Grenier (who was then aged about twenty) at the Franciscan house at Bordeaux, he gives a very full account of the wretched creature : " Il auoit les dents fort longues, claires, larges plus que le cōmun, et aucunement en dehors, gastees, et à demi noires, à force de se ruer sur les animaux, et sur les personnes : et les ongles aussi, longs, et aucuns tous noirs depuis la racine iusqu'au bout, mesme celuy du poulce de la main gauche, que le Diable luy auoit prohibé de rogner : et ceux qui estoiēt ainsi noirs, on eust dict qu'ils estoient à demy vsez et plus enfoncez que les autres, et plus hors leur naturel parce qu'il s'en seruoit plus que de ses pieds. Qui monstre clairement qu'il a faict le mestier de loup-garou, et qu'il vsoit de ses mains, et pour courir, et pour prēdre les enfans et les chiens à la gorge."

De Lancre justly considers the command of the demon to the effect that the werewolf must not cut the nail of his left thumb which grew long, horny, and hard as the talon of a beast, to be merely a piece of foul superstition, harmful in itself, as indicating a certain obedience to the Devil's tyranny even in small details. " Il monstre l'ongle du poulce gauche fort espoix et fort lōg, que le Diable luy a defendu de coupper, qui est vne pure folic en foy, mais marque de creance et obeissance au mauuais Demon, qui tient les couers bandez par telles superstitiōs." [156]

The signs upon which our author, than whom nobody perhaps, save the great Boguet, was more qualified to pronounce and had better opportunity of judging, insists upon most emphatically are the horrible eyes of the werewolf, " les yeux hagands, petits, enfoncez et noirs, tout esgarez," the mirrors of the bestial soul ; and also that the werewolf even in human form is unmistakably animal, " ayant tousiours gardé du bestial." [157]

This werewolf walked more easily on all fours than upright as a human being, and his agility in clambering and leaping limberly was almost supernatural. " Il auoit vne merueilleuse aptitude à aller à quatre pattes . . . et à sauter de forrez comme fort les animaux de quatre pieds." [158]

He was marked on the buttock with the Devil's mark, which spot upon his being first taken was altogether callous and insensible, though very plain to see ; but afterwards when he was reclaimed from his sorceries it gradually grew tender and soft, almost fading away and indiscernible. All werewolves—I do not speak of the involuntary ensorcelled transformation—are witches, and therefore all werewolves will be found to be branded with the Devil's mark.[159]

Among the Danes it was said that if the eyebrows met so as to form a bar across the brow this signified the man was a werewolf, which would seem to be an old wives' saw.[160] However, Professor Westermarck, in his *Ritual and Belief in Morocco*,[161] when speaking of the evil eye mentions that " Persons with deep-set eyes and those whose eyebrows are united over the bridge of the nose are considered particularly dangerous ".

The " rangen *wolfs-zagel* " or *wolfs-zagelchan* of which Grimm speaks belongs to the realm of nursery lore.[162]

De Lancre tells us that the reason why the Devil is more ready to change the sorcerer into a wolf rather than any other animal is owing to the ferocity of the natural wolf, who ravages and devours, who does more harm to man than any other marauder beast in his kind. Moreover, the wolf typifies the eternal enemy of the lamb, and by the Lamb is symbolized Our Lord and Saviour Jesus Christ.[163]

We are now in a position briefly to sum up the results of our inquiry, and to ask what it is permitted to believe concerning werewolfism or shape-shifting, the metamorphosis of men into animals.

In the first place, we say that all such transformations are effected by diabolical power. S. Lorenzo Guistiniani tells us in his *De spirituali et casto Uerbi et Animæ connubio* [164] that by black magic and the craft of Satan extraordinary wonders are wrought, although not true miracles, for true miracles are of God alone, and if He will He works by His Angels or through His Saints. In the history of holy Job we read that God permitted the Devil to have power over His servant : " And the Lord said to Satan, Behold he is in thy hand, but yet save his life." [165]

It must, however, always be remembered that there can be no metamorphosis, no transformation, which implies or involves any act of creation. Master Conrad Koellin, a famous Dominican professor of Ulon, writes in all reverence that Creation is the greatest act of God : *Maximum opus est creationis, in quo ex nihilo fit aliquid.*[166]

Creation belongs to God alone. But we may distinguish, as Bodin says in his refutation of Weyer : " Mais VViers s'est bien abusé de prēdre la creation pour la generation, & la generation pour la transmutation : la premiere est *de nihilo*, qui est propre au createur, la seconde est ex eo quod subsistit, qui s'appelle γένεσις, *in informarum generatione* : & la troisieme n'est pas *motus*, c'est à dire κίνησις, ains seulement vn changement, & alteration accidentale, c'est à dire ἀχλοίωσις & μεταβολὴ, demeurāt forme essentielle. Et par ainsi ce que le createur a vne fois creé, les creatures engendrent par succession & transformēt par la proprieté & puissance que Dieu leur a donnees, que Thomas d'Aquin appelle Vertu naturelle, parlant des esprits en c'este sorte, *Omnes angeli boni & mali habent ex uirtute naturali potestatem transformandi corpora nostra.* Or tous les anciēs depuis Homere, & tous ceux qui ont faict les procès aux Sorciers, qui ont souffert tel changemēt, sont d'accord que la raison, & forme essentielle demeure immuable comme nous auons dict en son lieu. C'est donc vne simple alteration de la forme accidentale & corporelle, & non pas vne vraye transformation." [167]

In fine, shape-shifting may be accomplished in three ways.

The first method is by a glamour caused by the demon, so that the man changed (either voluntarily or under the influence of a spell) will seem both to himself and to all who behold him to be metamorphosed into the shape of a certain animal, and although, if it be a spell which has been cast upon him, he retains his human reason he cannot exercise the power of speech. The authors of the *Malleus Maleficarum* tell us that such transmutations are " proved by authority, by reason, and by experience ".[168] It was this metamorphosis which the father of Praestantius suffered when he thought he was a pack-horse and carried corn, whose story S. Augustine relates in the *De Ciuitate Dei*, xviii, 18. And the young merchant who was ensorcelled by the witch of Salamis and seemingly became an ass endured the same glamorous transformation. There are many other similar examples recorded, and to this demoniacal hallucination Remy [169] would refer most, if not all, cases of werewolfism; as I think, wrongly. The authors of the *Malleus Maleficarum* are of opinion that this matter of shape-shifting was Nabuchodonosor's case. As for the luggage and bales, which were loaded upon the sumpter-horse and the metamorphosed ass, they explain " that devils invisibly bore those burdens up when they were too heavy to be carried ".[170]

Henri Boguet allows another mode, for he writes : " My own opinion is that Satan sometimes leaves the witch asleep behind a bush, and himself goes and performs that which the witch has in mind to do, giving himself the appearance of a wolf; but that he so confuses the wolf's imagination that he believes he has really been a wolf and has run about and killed men and beasts . . . And when it happens that they find themselves wounded, it is Satan who immediately transfers to them the blow which he has received in his assumed body." [171] " When the witch is not bodily present at all," says Guazzo,[172] " then the Devil wounds her in that part of her absent body corresponding to the wound which he knows to have been received by the beast's body." We have here then a complete explanation of the phenomenon of repercussion, namely, that if the werewolf be wounded or maimed the witch will be found to be instantaneously wounded in numerically the same spot or maimed of the identical corresponsive limb, a piece of evidence which occurs again and again in the trials of lycanthropes. Guazzo tells us that on these occasions the demon " assumes the body of a wolf formed from the air and wrapped about him ",[173] whilst other authorities rather hold that the demon actually possesses some wolf. But whichever it be, this detail skills not. Moreover, as the learned Capuchin, Jacques d'Autun, teaches us,[174] even if this method be employed in shape-shifting, and the sorcerer is thrown into a mesmeric trance, whilst the familiar prowls abroad, the consenting witch is none the less guilty of the murders and ravages wrought by the demon in lupine form, and by very force of his evil pact with hell he cannot in any whit disculpate himself from the shedding of blood and bestial savagery.

This method of werewolfism and metamorphosis, although infrequent, is amply proven. It does not, however, account for the immense weariness felt by the sorcerer after his animal expeditions and courses of the night. When treating of a similar matter, Remy, in his *Demonolatry*, book i, chapter xxiv,[175] explains how *The Transvection of Men through the Air by Good Angels, of which we read in Time past, was calm and free from Labour ; but that by which Witches are now transported by Demons is full of Pain and Weariness.* By the very confessions of the witches themselves it was acknowledged that when the demon " carries his disciples through the air in this manner, he leaves them far more heavily overcome with weariness than if they had completed a rough journey afoot with the greatest urgency ". Father Jacques d'Autun points out that the cases when the sorcerer is thrown into a coma, and the ravages of lycanthropy are impressed upon his imaginative faculty by the demon, so that he supposes himself as a wolf actually to have been galloping tantivy over hill and dale, through forest and bosky dingle, are very rare ; and to attribute the decrepit lassitude of the werewolf merely to the sick fantasy of a nightmare cannot but be regarded as inconsequential and vain.[176]

The third method by which shape-shifting may be accomplished, and that which from accumulated evidence would seem to be immeasurably the more general mode of werewolfism and other devilish transformation, cannot be better described than in the words of Guazzo : " Sometimes, in accordance with his pact, the demon surrounds a witch with an aerial effigy of a beast, each part of which fits on to the correspondent part of the witch's body, head to head, mouth to mouth, belly to belly, foot to foot, and arm to arm ; but this only happens when they use certain ointments and words. . . . In this last case it is no matter for wonder if they are afterwards found with an actual wound in those parts of their human body where they were wounded when in the appearance of a beast ; for the enveloping air easily yields, and the true body receives the wound." [177]

" I maintain," says Boguet, " that for the most part it is
the witch himself who runs about slaying : not that he is
metamorphosed into a wolf, but that it appears to him that
he is so." A little later he adds, after having reviewed the
confessions of the lycanthropes at their trial : " Who now
can doubt but that these witches themselves ran about and
committed the acts and murders of which we have spoken ?
For what was the cause of the fatigue they experienced ?
If they had been sleeping behind some bush, how did they
become fatigued ? What caused the scratches on their
persons, if it was not the thorns and bushes through which
they ran in their pursuit of man and animals ? " " They
confessed also that they tired themselves with running."
Clauda Jamprost, a horrible hag, old and lame, when asked
how it happened that she was able to clamber over rocks
and boulders in the swift midnight venery, answered that
she was borne along by Satan. " But this in no way renders
them immune from fatigue."

On one occasion Benoist Bidel, a lad of fifteen or sixteen,
had climbed a tree to pluck some fruit, leaving his younger
sister at the foot. The girl was attacked by a wolf, who
suddenly darted from the bushes, whereupon her brother
quickly descending endeavoured to protect her. The wolf,
turning to the boy, with a fierce blow of its paw drove into
his neck a knife he was carrying. By this time a number
of people had rushed to the assistance of the children and
beat off the animal, maiming and hurting it. The lad was
carried into his father's house, where he died of his wounds
in a few days. But before he died he declared that the wolf
which had torn him had its two forefeet like a man's hands
covered on the top with hair. There expired, maimed and
injured (although nobody exactly knew how) precisely as
the wolf had been hurt, a woman in the village, who was a
notorious witch, Perrenette Gandillon. They then realized
that it was she who had killed the boy.

Similarly, when Jeanne Perrin was going through a wood
with Clauda Gaillard, Clauda, grumbling that she had received
so few alms, darted into the bushes and there came out a
huge wolf. Jeanne Perrin, crossing herself and letting fall
the alms she had collected, ran away in terror, for she swore
that this wolf had toes on its hind feet like a human being.

There is a strong presumption that this wolf was no other than Clauda Gaillard, for she afterwards told Jeanne that the wolf which attacked her would not have done her any harm.[178]

These then are instances when the human figure was hideously breaking through the animal envelope. Precisely the same thing happened in the case of Gilles Garnier, who was condemned at Dôle in January, 1573,[179] a circumstance attested by many creditable witnesses.

In some instances the demon supplied the sorcerer with an envelope of wolf-skins, but the effect was the same. As we have already seen, the werewolf Jean Grenier possessed a pelt of this description.

Not without reason did the werewolf in past centuries appear as one of the most terrible and depraved of all bond-slaves of Satan. He was even whilst in human form a creature within whom the beast—and not without prevailing—struggled with the man. Masqued and clad in the shape of the most dreaded and fiercest denizen of the forest the witch came forth under cover of darkness, prowling in lonely places, to seek his prey. By the force of his diabolic pact he was enabled, owing to a ritual of horrid ointments and impious spells, to assume so cunningly the swift shaggy brute that save by his demoniac ferocity and superhuman strength none could distinguish him from the natural wolf. The werewolf loved to tear raw human flesh. He lapped the blood of his mangled victims, and with gorged reeking belly he bore the warm offal of their palpitating entrails to the sabbat to present in homage and foul sacrifice to the Monstrous Goat who sat upon the throne of worship and adoration. His appetites were depraved beyond humanity. In bestial rut he covered the fierce she-wolves amid their bosky lairs. If he were attacked and sore wounded, if a limb, a paw or ear were lopped, perforce he must regain his human shape, and he fled to some cover to conceal these fearful transformations, where man broke through the shell of beast in horrid confusion. The human body was maimed or wounded in that numerical place where the beast had been hurt. By this were his bedevilments not unseldom betrayed, he was recognized and brought to justice. Hateful to God and loathed of man, what other end, what other reward could he look for than the stake, where they burned him quick, and scattered his ashes to the wind, to be swept away to nothingness and oblivion on the keen wings of the tramontane and the nightly storm.

FOOTNOTES:

[1] *A Monograph of the Canidae*, 1890, by St. George Mivart, F.R.S., pp. 3–83. This book gives nine exceedingly fine hand-coloured plates of different varieties of wolves. See also *Fur-Bearing Animals*, by Henry Poland, F.Z.S., 1892, pp. 65–76. St. George Mivart is my principal authority for the natural history of the wolf.

[2] *Zoologische Garten*, xxiv, *Jahrgang* (1883), p. 91. See further, *Archives Cosmologiques*, Bruxelles, 1868, p. 78, plate 5. (A black wolf killed near Dinant, Belgium, in 1868.) Also E. Griffith, F.S.A., *Animal Kingdom* (Cuvier's *Le règne animal*), 15 vols., 1827–1832 ; vol. ii, p. 348.

[3] *Coelii Rhodogini Lectiones Antiquae*, folio, 1666, p. 1185. Ulisse Aldrovandi, *De Quadrupedibus Solidipedibus*, folio, Bononiae, 1616, pp. 118–19. Vergil, *Georgics*, iii, 206–8, speaking of horses.

[4] Poland, op. cit., p. 67.

[5] Holland's translation, folio, 1601, vol. i, p. 207.

[6] *Genesis*, xlix, 27, " Benjamin, a ravenous wolf," whom Cornelius à Lapide, *In Pentateuchum*, Antverpiae, folio, 1616, p. 299, compares to " Romulum rapacem . . . eo quod lacte lupae esset nutritus ". *Ecclesiasticus*, xiii, 12 ; *Jeremias*, v, 6 ; *Ezechiel*, xxii, 27 ; *Sophonias*, iii, 8.

[7] *Lupus quis* ? Lupus primo est haereticus. Secundo, quiuis sceleratus, qui fideles uerbo, uel exemplo rapere et peruertere studet [ut puta modernista]. Tertio, lupus est diabolus." A Lapide, *In Ioannem*, x, 12. *In IV Euangelia*, Lugduni, folio, 1638, ii, p. 402.

[8] " Nonne lupis istis haeretici comparandi sunt ? " *Expositio Euangel. sec. Lucam*, lib. vii, c. x, 3. Migne, *Patres Lat.*, xv, col. 1711 (49).

[9] Chaucer, *Complete Works*, ed. Skeat. One vol., Oxford, n.d., p. 703 (*Sequitur de Auaricia*, 67). *English Register of Godstow Nunnery*, ed. A. Clarke, 1905, part i. (The holy martyrs Cyriac and Julitta, his mother, under Diocletian, *Roman Martyrology*, 16th June.) John Alcock, Bishop of Rochester, 1430–1500. The Hill of Perfection was printed 1491, 1497, and 1501. Kendall, *Epigrammes*, 8vo, 1577, 43.

[10] *Iliad* iv, 471–2 ; xi, 70–3 ; xvi, 351–7. Among Homeric epithets of wolves are πολίοι, grisly ; ὠμοφάγοι, devourers of raw red meat ; κρατερώνυχες, with strong sharp claws ; ὀρέστεροι, brood of the mountains. Æschylus, *Septem*, 1035, terms them κοιλογάστορες, with void ravening bellies. Cf. the English " hungry as a wolf ", as in John Palgrave's *Acolastus*, 1540, iii, 3, when the parasite Pamphagus says : " Nam uel lupo esurientior Sum," and Palgrave has, " I am more hungry thā any wolfe is " (sig. L). Cf. again, " to keep the wolf from the door," as " he maye the wolf werre from the gate ", Hardyng's *Chronicon* (c. 1470), and in *Institutions of a Gentleman*, 1555, sig. G. i, " keping yᵉ wulf from the doore (as they cal it)." Also John Goodman, *The Penitent Pardoned* (1679), seventh ed., 1713, i, 11, p. 31. The word wolf is applied to a ravenous appetite, as in Gesner's *Jewell of Health*.

For the Latin phrase *Lupus in fabula* (or *sermone*), an adage used when such a one who had been recently spoken of arrived abruptly on the scene, see Plautus, *Stichus*, iv, 1, 71, also the *Adelphi*, iv, 1, 21, with the gloss of Donatus who gives rather a different turn to the phrase. Also see Thomas Wilson, *The Art of Rhetorique*, ed. 1580, p. 202 : " We saie Whiste, the Woulfe is at hande, when the same man cometh in the meane season, of whom we spake before."

For a dilemma, " lupum auribus tenere," *Phormio*, iii, 11, 21, and the gloss of Donatus. Marlowe, *Edward II* (1594), 2115–17, Mortimer to Isabel :—
> For now we hould an old Wolfe by the eares,
> That if he slip will seaze vpon vs both,
> And gripe the sorer, being gript himselfe.

Quarles, *Samson*, xi, 63 (1631). For a difficult job, " lupo agnum eripere," *Poenulus*, iii, 5, 81. Cf. " To be in the wolf's mouth," " à la gueule du loup," for deadly peril. " There was Eilred in the wolfes mouth," Robert Mannyng of Brunne, *Chronicle*, ed. 1810, p. 42. Erasmus in his *Adagia* has noted several interesting and important proverbial references to the wolf. Ælian says the wolf is the fiercest and most malevolent of all animals, *De Nat. Animal.*, ed. Hercher, Paris, Didot, 1858, vii, 20. He is a harpy, unclean. Ibid., *Fragmentum 354*, p. 470. He is baleful, accursed, something wholly evil, Aristophanes of Byzantium, *Historiae Animalium Epitome*, ii, 235–244, ed. Spyridion P. Lambros, vol. i, par. 1. *Supplementum Aristotelicum*, Berolini, 1885, pp. 89–90.

[11] Beaumont and Fletcher, *The Custome of the Countrey*, folio, 1647, iv, where Rutilio speaks of " these unsatisfied Men-leeches, women ".

[12] Aristaenetus, Ep., ii, 20. " ὡς γὰρ λύκοι τοὺς ἄρνας ἀγαπῶσιν, οὕτω τὰ γύναια ποθοῦσιν οἱ νέοι, καὶ λυκοφιλία τούτων ὁ πόθος." *Epistolographi Graeci*, ed. W. Hercher, Didot, Paris, 1873, p. 170.

[13] 241 D.

[14] The couplet is from Taylor's translation of the *Phaedrus*, 1792 (anon.), p. 42.

[15] *Anthologia Graeca*, xi (Musa Puerilis), 250, ed. Didot, Parisiis, 1872, vol. ii, p. 429.

[16] *The Greek Anthology, Epigrams from Anthologia Palatina XII*. Translated into English verse by Sydney Oswald. Privately issued, 1914, p. 21, " Drunken Vows."

[17] iv, 19. Frankfort, 1608, p. 209. See also the edition by Dindorf, Lipsiae, 1834, 5 vols., vol. iv, p. 822. " τὰ δὶ γυναικῶν πρόσωπα εἴη τοιαῦτα. γρᾳδίον ἰσχνὸν ἢ λυκαίνιον . . . τὸ μὲν λυκαίνιον ὑπόμηκες ῥυτίδες λεπταὶ καὶ πυκναί. λευκὸν, ὕπωχρον, στρεβλὸν τὸ ὄμμα." *Pollucis Onamasticon*, ed. Eric Bethe, Lipsiae (Teubner), мсм, p. 245.

[18] 55 (54), 11.

[19] Auctore P.P., Parisiis, 1826, p. 295. See also *Supplementum et Index Lexicorum Eroticorum Linguae Latinae*, Paris, 1911, pp. 176–7.

[20] iii, 1, 12.

[21] Lugd. Bat. Apud Franciscum Hackium et Petrum Lessen, 1660 ; pp. 101–2.

[22] " The most famous of all (homosexual romances) remains to be recorded. This is the story of Harmodius and Aristegeiton, who freed Athens from the tyrant Hipparchus. There is not a speech, a poem, or essay, a panegyrical oration in praise of either Athenian liberty or Greek love which does not tell the tale of this heroic friendship. Herodotus and Thucydides treat the event as a matter of serious history. Plato refers to it as the beginning of freedom for the Athenians. The drinking-song in honour of these lovers is one of the most precious fragments of popular Greek poetry which we possess. . . . Harmodius and Aristegeiton were reverenced as martyrs and saviours of their country. Their names gave consecration to the love which made them bold against the despot, and they became at Athens eponyms of paiderastia." J. A. Symonds, *A Problem in Greek Ethics*, p. 179, *Sexual Inversion*, by Havelock Ellis and John Addington Symonds, 1897.

[23] Pausanias, i, 28, 2 ; Plutarch, *De Ganulitate*, 8 ; Polynaeus, viii, 45. Pliny, *Nat. H.*, xxxiv, 72 ; Clement of Alexandria, *Stromata*, iv, 19, 122, ed. Potter, p. 618 ; Athenaeus, xiii ; Lactantius, i, 20. Athenaeus represents Leaena as the mistress of Harmodius ; Pausanias and Polynaeus name her as the mistress of Aristegeiton. These accounts are incorrect. She was mistress of neither of the lovers.

[24] Ed. Amstelædami, Apud Henricum Wetstenium, 1684, p. 69.

[25] The Commentary on Ausonius of the great French Scholar Élie Vinet

(1509–1587) is much esteemed. His Ausonius was first printed 8° 1575, and again 8° 1590, 8° 1604, etc. I have used the Amsterdam Ausonius, 1671, " Apud Ioannem Blaev," p. 23.

²⁶ ll. 107–8. Migne, *P.L.*, lx, p. 126. The old gloss on l. 107 has Lupas, *meretrices*. Barthius cites an old codex for a reading " ruricolas " and suggests (quite needlessly) " lustricolas " in this passage.

²⁷ The author of this work was Nicolas Chorier, who was born at Vienna in 1609, and died in 1692, highly honoured for his scholarship and literary genius. He ascribed his erotic masterpiece, first published in 1649, to Luisa Sigea, an erudite Spanish lady, who was born about 1530 and died at Burgos in 1560. She was often termed in compliment the Minerva of her age.

The *Satyra sotadica* is represented as having been translated into Latin by Jean Meursius, the celebrated antiquary, 1623–1653, son of the more famous Jean Meursius.

It is said that M. Rochas possessed a key to the interlocutors of the Satire. " La *Satire* de Chorier est un chef-d'œuvre et l'on ne saurait trop louer . . . cet art suprême de varier merveilleusement un sujet limité."

²⁸ Acted before Pope Leo X in the Rucellai Gardens on the occasion of a Papal visit to Florence.

²⁹ *Joannis Palegravi Londoniensis Ecphrasis Anglica in Comoediam Acolasti*, 1540. Lond. in aedibus Tho. Berthel (sig. x).

³⁰ Schwenck, *Sinn bilden der alten Völker*, p. 524.

³¹ A few references in Greek and Latin literature to the wolf as an omen of ill may serve for many. Pausanias, ix, 18, 4 (Battle of Leuctra) ; i, 19, 6 ; i, 41, 3 ; v, 15, 8 ; vii, 26, 3 and 11 ; viii, 32, 4. Livy, iii, 29, 9 ; xxi, 46, 1–2 ; xxi, 62, 5 ; xxii, 1, 12 ; xxvii, 37, 3 (sentinel at Capua killed by midnight wolf) ; xxxii, 29 ; xxxiii, 26, 8–9 ; xli, 9, 6 ; see also Julius Obsequens, *De Prodigiis*, ed. C. H. Hase, Parisiis, 1823, xvii (p. 44) ; xxv (p. 47) ; ciii (p. 184) ; and cix (p. 48). F. B. Krauss, *An Interpretation of the Omens, Portents, and Prodigies recorded by Livy, Tacitus, and Suetonius*, Philadelphia, 1930, attempts a rationalistic explanation of the phenomena, and is singularly inconclusive and unsatisfactory. See also Zonaras for Mark Antony at Brundisium, *Annales* ex recensione Mauricii Pinderi, Bonnae, 1844, ii, pp. 376–7 (*Corpus Scriptorum Historiae Byzantinae*). Also Horace, *Carm.* iii, xxvii, 1–4. Also Aratus, *Geoponika*, i, 3, and xv, 1 (Eng. tr. T. Owen, 1805, vol. ii, p. 190). For curious wolf lore one may consult Antoine Mizauld, *Centuriae IX Memorabilium*, 1566 ; ed. 1592, Cent. i, 24 (p. 7) ; Cent. viii, 5 (p. 164) ; et alibi. See also Pliny, *Hist. Nat.*, xxviii, 10 and 20.

³² Phytognomonica, iii, 18 ; Neapoli, 1588, p. 113.

³³ *Cædwalla*, London, Seeley and Co., 1888, ch. iv, p. 55.

³⁴ *Norimbergae apud J. Petreium*, folio. Also the same year (1550) Lugduni.

³⁵ Basiliae, folio, 1557, pp. 498–9.

³⁶ *Naturall Historie*, Holland, folio, 1601. The first tome, p. 207, viii, 22.

³⁷ Parisiis, 1583, p. 41.

³⁸ Ed. J. G. Reiff, 2 vols., Lipsiae, 1805. Vol. i, p. 159. See also Ulisse Aldrovandi, *De Quadrupedibus Digitatis Uiuiparis*, Bologna, folio, 1637, i, pp. 164–5.

³⁹ For further wolf lore see Philip Camerarius, *Operae Horarum Subcisiuarum*, Centuria altera, cap. 90 ; Alessandro Alessandri, *Geniales Dies*, v, xiii ; Giampietro Valeriano of Belluno, *Hieroglyphica*, Basle, 1566, xi (ed. Basileæ, 1575, pp. 79–82). Camerarius has the story of Gelon of Syracuse and the kindly wolf. Antigonus of Carystus in his *Historiae Mirabiles* tells how wolves guard the tackle of fishermen living on the shores of Lake Maeotis (Azor), and how the animals are fed as a reward for their pains.

⁴⁰ Ed. Spyridion P. Lambros, *Supplementum Aristotelicum*, vol. i, Berolini, 1885, p. 90.

⁴¹ Ed. James Britton, Folk-Lore Soc., London, 1881, p. 115 and p. 204.

⁴² *Zeitschrift fur Romanische Philologie*, xxxii (1908): " Sizilianische Gebete, Beschwörungen und Rezepte in griechischer Umschrift," Heinrich Schneeguns, pp. 571–594.

[43] I quote from folio, 1635, as a fuller text, pp. 13–14. Of 1629 Bodley has a fine—perhaps a unique—copy, formerly in the library of that great bibliophile James Crossley (Antiq. c. E. $\frac{1627}{1}$).

[44] *The Works of Virgil*, folio, 1697 ; Pastoral ix, 74–5 ; p. 43. There are constant references to this belief. Plato, *Laws*, x, 906, says that dogs may be charmed to silence by the wolf's gaze. See Pliny, viii, 22 ; S. Ambrose, *Expos. Euang. sec. Lucam*, vii, 48 (Migne, *P.L.*, xiv, col. 1711)); Themistus, Oratio XXI, ed. Petavius, Parisiis, fol., 1684, p. 253 ; *Geoponika*, xv, 1 ; Vincent of Beauvais, *Speculum Doctrinale*, Lib. xvii, cap. 92 (fol. Venice, 1591, tom. ii, p. 270) ; William of Auvergne, *De Uniuerso*, II, i, cap. 32 (*Opera Omnia*, Venetiis, 1591, p. 786); S. Isidore, *Etymologies*, xii (*P.L.*, lxxxii, col. 438) ; Le Loyer, *Des Spectres*, I, viii (Angers, 1586, pp. 206–7), where he derives *Coqueluche* from κακὰ λύκου. Cotgrave (1611) defines Coqueluche as a " *new disease, which troubled the French about the yeares 1550, and 1557 ; and us but a while ago* ". See also Vair, *De Fascino*, i, 1 and i, 3 (ed. 1583, p. 5 and p. 14) ; Thomas of Cantimpre, *De Apibus*, ii, cap. 57 ; Cardano, *De Subtilitate*, lib. xviii (ed. Basileæ, 1557, pp. 498–9) ; Delrio, *Disquisit. Mag.*, i, cap. iii, q. 4. Sennert, *De Morbis Occultis* (Opera om. 1641, t. i, p. 1130), derides the tradition. Robert de Triez, *Ruses, Finesses et Impostures des Esprits Maleris*, Cambrai, 1563, p. 28 *uerso*, upholds the belief " si le loup descouure de preme veue l'hôme, il le rēd enroué et le priue de voix et de parolle ". See also Basile, Pentamerone, Jorn. I, tratt. viii, ed. 1788, tom. i, p. 84 ; Tasso, *Aminta*, i, 2 ; and Marino, *L'Adone*, xii, 75.

[45] In later editions *si le Diable peut* became *si les esprits peuuent*.

[46] For the teaching of S. Thomas see particularly *Supra IV Libros Sententiarum*, liber ii, Distinct. septima et Distinct. octaua, ed. Parisiis, 1574, pp. 212–19.

[47] *Malleus Maleficarum*, tr. Montague Summers, folio, 1928, p. 148.

[48] *Wunderzeichen, Warhafftige Beschreibung und gründlich verzeicnus schrecklicker Wunderzeichen und Geschichten, die von . . . MDXVII bis auff . . . MDLVI geschehn und ergangen sind, noch der Jarzal . . .* Jhena, 8vo, 1556.

[49] *Malleus*, ut sup., pp. 126–7.

[50] c. 1517–1564. Belon in chapter lii (ed. Paris, 4to, 1554, pp. 120–1) writes *Des Basteleries qu'on Faict au Caire*.

[51] *Speculum Naturale*, lib. ii, cap. cix. The incident, which I relate at length in Chapter III, occurred under Pope S. Leo IX, 1049–1054.

[52] *De Ciu. Dei*, XVIII, xviii.

[53] pp. 137–140.

[54] Ed. Francofurti, 1602, p. 328.

[55] First ed., Paris, folio, 1548. I have used the Æditio Secunda, Paris, fol., 1551, pp. 159–161. Jean Fernel, " the modern Galen," 1497–1558.

[56] pp. 172–185.

[57] Binsfeld, *De Confessionibus Maleficorum*, 3 Conclusio, ed. Aug. Treu. 1605, pp. 194–5, mentions Ulrich Molitor, and adds " male eum Bodinus pro se allegat ".

[58] Dom Paul Piolin, *Gallia Christiana*, tom. ii (Paris, 1873), 1200–1. Ibid., 1080. Bishop Louis Guerinet was translated to Fréjus about 1462, see *Gallia Christiana*, tom. i (Paris, 1870), 439–40.

[59] Cap. xxvi. Migne, *P.L.*, xl, col. 798.

[60] pp. 694–5.

[61] Regino of Prüm, *Libri Duo de Synodalibus Causis et Disciplinis Ecclesiasticis*, ii, 371, ed. Wasserschleben, 1840, pp. 354–6. The text is conveniently given by Hansen, *Geschichte des Hexenwahns*, Bonn, 1894, pp. 38–9.

[62] Policraticus, ii, 17, ed. Webb, i, 100–1.

[63] *De Natura Daemonum*, Venice, 8vo, 1581, iv, 4.

[64] Libro Primo, capitolo ix. " Si mostra l'identità della Società Dianiana colla moderna Streghiera, e si esamina il *Can. Episcopi* 26. q. 5," pp. 50–63.

[65] pp. 380–1.

⁶⁶ Francofurti, 1581, "summo studio Fr. Joan. Myntrenberg Carmeliti," pp. 61–72.

⁶⁷ Malleus Maleficarum ; Daemonastrix ; 1669, t. iii, p. 183.

⁶⁸ Migne, Patres Graeci, lvii, col. 353.

⁶⁹ Opera omnia, ed. by the Quaracchi Fathers, tom. ii (1885, pp. 200–4).

⁷⁰ Ibid., pp. 227–230.

⁷¹ Folio, Cologne, 1622, tom. ii, pp. 147–151. See further, Relationes Undecim of Fra Francisco Vittoria, O.P., Salamantiae, 1565, "De Arte Magica," pp. 350–385 ; and François Garassus, S.J., Somme Théologique, folio, Paris, 1625, pp. 915–18, for a discussion of Signum, Prodigium, Monstrum, Miraculum.

⁷² Venice, 1523. I have used the ed., Coloniae, 1581, pp. 54–9.

⁷³ Holie Bible. Doway, 1610. Vol. ii, p. 784. Daniel, iv, 30. Lambert Daneau in Les Sorciers translated as A Dialogue of Witches by Thomas Taylor, 1575, in his discussion of shape-shifting, chapter iii (sig. F. i), says that "it is thus to be understoode of Nabucadnezer, that we must not thinke that his humane nature was conuerted into the essencil or being of a brute beast. But his conuersation was chaunged, and his mynde and affection". Daneau has nothing new to offer in his consideration of metamorphosis but is trivial to a degree with his easy prattle of "meere tryfles and oulde wyues tales ".

⁷⁴ Eng. tr. by Montague Summers, folio, London, 1928, pp. 61–5.

⁷⁵ De fantasia, capitulum sextum. "Operatur etiam angelus malus, id est diabolus circa fantasiam hominis ad decipiendum." S. Antoninus cites the examples of S. Macharius and Simon Magus. He also examines the Canon Episcopi. He teaches that the Devil effects these wonders "alterando fantasias hominum. Cum autem potentia fantastica siue imaginatiua sit corporalis id est affixa organo corporeo, naturaliter est subdita angelis malis ut possint ea transmutare". Of the Summa of S. Antoninus I have used the Venice folio, 1487.

⁷⁶ Albertus Magnus : De Animalibus Libri XXVI, ed. Hermann Stadler, Band i, Münster, 1916 ; Band ii, Münster, 1921. (Beitrage zur Geschichte der Philosophie des Mittelalters, Band xv, Band xvi.)

⁷⁷ Part ii, question 1, chapter 8 deals with the Manner whereby (Witches) Change Men into the Shape of Beasts. Eng. tr., pp. 122–4.

⁷⁸ Remy, Demonolatry, book ii, ch. 5, Eng. tr., London, 1929, pp. 108–114 ; Guazzo, Compendium Maleficarum, book i, ch. 13, Eng. tr., 1929, pp. 50–8 ; Boguet, Examen of Witches, chap. 47, Eng. tr., 1929, pp. 186–155.
In his Daemonomagia, Frankfort, 1607, quaestio xii, pp. 153–4, Philip Ludwig Elich has some valuable remarks upon werewolfery. He refers to "quodam λυκανθρώπῳ, cui nomen Peter Stumpff", and he mentions the terms "Beer-Wolff, nobis uerius atque magis proprie Teuffelswolff, Graecis λυκανθρώπους et μυρμολυκίας, siue ἀρκτολύκους".

⁷⁹ Typis . . . Monasterii S. Galli, Anno MDCXC, 2 vols., folio. Vol. i, p. 112. Sub anno 1470. Baianus is spoken of as one who "in arte Magica peritissimus omnium suo tempore mortalium habebatur", cf. p. 120. "Daemonum cooperatione mutauisse non dubium a nescientibus praestigiorum eius rationem occultam putabatur." All such wonders are termed "daemonum ludibria ".

⁸⁰ Fourth ed., Leucoreis Athenis (Wittenberg), 1613, pp. 263–4.

⁸¹ De Sagarum Natura et Potestate, Deq.; His Recte Cognoscendis Et Puniendis Physiologia Gulielmi Adolphi Scribonii Marpurgensis. Ubi De Purgatione Earum per aquam frigidam. Marpurgi, 1588. "De Sagarum in catos, feles, aliaue eiuscemodi animantia transformatione," pp. 66–77. For Scribonius see N. F. J. Eloy, Dictionnaire Historique de la Médicine, t. iv (1778), p. 286.

⁸² Paris, 1578, ch. xiv, pp. 26–7.

⁸³ Trèves, 8vo, 1591. (Éd. Trèves, 8vo, 1605, pp. 193–204.}

⁸⁴ Col. Agrippinae, 1594, pp. 111–136. "De Prodigiosis Uiuorum Apparitionibus sub Peregrina et Bestiarum Forma."

⁸⁵ Folio, Moguntiae, 1603, pp. 163–6.

⁸⁶ Paris, 1605, pp. 184–145.

[87] Wittenberg, 1606, pp. 22–6.

[88] pp. 496–517.

[89] Privilège, 1 Dec., 1595.

[90] Nabuchodonosor, King of Babylon ; Daniel, iv, 23–34. For a discussion of the lycanthropy of Nabuchodonosor see Dr. Pusey's lectures, *Daniel the Prophet*, 1864, pp. 425–437 ; also M. l'abbé Henri Lesètre, curé of Saint-Etienne-du-Mont, Paris, article *Folie* in the *Dictionnaire de la Bible*, F. Vigouroux, Paris, 1899, fasc. xv, 2301–2 ; Brière de Boismont, *Des hallucinations*, Paris, 1852, p. 383 ; Petrus Archidiaconus, *Quaestiones in Danielem*, Migne, *P.L.*, xcvi, coll. 1549–50 ; Nicolas de Lyra, *Bibliorum Sacrorum . . . Postilla Nicolai Lyrani*, folio, Lugduni, 1589, tom. iv, 1553–6 ; Michael Medina, *De Fide*, ii, 7 ; Cornelius à Lapide, *Comm. in Danielem*, Antverpiae, folio, 1621, pp. 45–7 ; Girolamo Mercuriale, *Medicina Practica*, i, xii, *De Lykanthropia*, fol., Francofurti, 1601, pp. 56–7 ; Dom Augustin Calmet, *Dissertation sur la Metamorphose de Nabuchodonosor*, in his *Commentaire Littéral sur tous les Livres de l'Ancien et de Nouveau Testament*, Paris, 25 vols., 1709–1716, vol. xiv (1715), pp. 542–555. The Danish Archbishop, Joannes Suaningius, in his *Commentarium in Danielem*, 2 vols., folio, Hanniae, 1564, vol. i, pp. 503–4, is frankly rationalistic, and Dr. Richard Mead in his *Medica Sacra*, 1749, cap. vii, is of the same temper. For the Rabbinical traditions concerning Nabuchodonosor, which are very curious, see S. Jerome, Migne, *P.L.*, xxv, col. 1300–2 ; *Biblia Sacra Lyrani*, Lugd., 1589, vol. iv, 2058–9 ; Cornelius à Lapide, *In XII Prophetas Minores*, Lugd., 1625, *In Habacuc*, cap. ii, 15, 16, pp. 61–2.

[91] *Le manuel de l'admirable victoire du corps du Dieu sur l'esprit maling Beelzebub obtenue à Laon* 1566, by Iehan Boulæse, Paris, 16mo, 1575.

[92] Privilège, 9 Avril, 1615.

[93] *Holie Bible*, Doway, 1609, i, p. 177. Exodus, viii, 6, 7.

[94] F. *Baptistae Mantuani Carm. Theo. Fastorum Libri XII.* Argentorati, 1518.

[95] London, Redway, 1887, pp.258–263.

[96] *A Digest of the Writings of Éliphas Lévi*, by A. E. Waite ; London, 1886, pp. 218–220.

[97] *Theosophical Manuals*, No. 3. Third ed. (revised). London, Theo. Pub. Soc., 1900, pp. 58–61.

[98] London, 1865.

[99] London, 1912. Chapter i, pp. 14–15.

[100] A few names may perhaps be briefly mentioned in a note. Voltaire in the *Dictionnaire philosophique* (under *Enchantement*) thought a young shepherd dressed in a wolf's skin settled the whole question. J. G. Keysler in his *Antiquates Selectae Septentrionales et Celticae*, Hanover, 1720, pp. 494–7, has no better suggestion to offer than Crusaders' tales from the East. J. G. Wachter, *Glossarium Germanicum*, Lipsiae, 1737, under *Werwolf* (pp. 1880–2), appears to attribute the belief in werewolfism to some ritual dressing in pelts and furs. Dunlop in his *History of Fiction*, 1814 (new ed., H. Wilson, 1888, Bohn, vol. ii, pp. 542–3), thought that werewolfery " had its foundation in the imposition of pretended sorcerers ", a hint which was eagerly seized upon by Sir E. B. Tylor in his *Primitive Culture* (fourth ed., London, 1903, vol. i, p. 312), who wrote airily enough, as anthropologists wont, of " the tricks of magicians ". De Gubernatis (*Zoological Mythology*, Eng. tr., 2 vols., 1872 ; vol. ii, p. 145) saw in lycanthropy " the zoological transformations of the solar hero ", whatever that may mean. Canon MacCulloch in his *Mediaeval Faith and Fable*, London, 1932 (chapter v, Shape-Shifting), regards " werewolves as lunatics who imagined that they were wolves ". If I read him aright he denies any " diabolic influence in the mental delusion ". This is not surprising since this study, most painful in its frank scepticism, seems throughout almost entirely to reject the supernatural. Canon MacCulloch has a lengthy article, " Lycanthropy," in the *Encyclopædia of Religion and Ethics* (Hastings), vol. viii, 216. The writers in the *Encyclopædia Britannica*, eleventh ed., 1911 (article " Lycanthropy " by N. W. Thomas,

vol. xvii, pp. 149–50, and article " Werwolf ", vol. xxviii, pp. 524–6, N. W. Thomas and J. F. M'Lennan), do not arrive at any definite conclusions concerning these dark problems. Ritual anthropophagy, arising and developed from some forgotten totemic belief, is the fanciful postulate of Mr. Lewis Spence, who seems to be misled by the whimsey that witchcraft was a survival of a so-called " Dianic cult ", " The Cult of the Werwolf in Europe," *Occult Review*, Oct., 1921, vol. xxxiv, No. 4, pp. 221–6.

[101] For instances see : *Malleus Maleficarum*, part ii, qn. 1, ch. 8 (Eng. tr., pp. 122–4) ; Remy, ii, 5 (Eng. tr., pp. 108–14) ; Binsfeld, *De Confessionibus Maleficarum*, 3 Conclusio (ed. 1605, pp. 193–204) ; Vincent of Beauvais, *Speculum naturale*, ii, cix (Venice, fo., 1591, tom. i, p. 26) ; Baptista Fulgosi, *Dictorum Factorumque Mirabilium*, viii, xi, " Recentiora " (folio, Basle, 1555, p. 989) ; Prierias, *De strigimagibus*, ii, viii, Ed. 1521, Romae, pp. 105 (uerso)–109, actually the pages are not numbered, Sigs. cc ii–dd ii ; Pico de Mirandola, *Strix . . . Dialogi tres*, ed. Argentorati, 1612, pp. 81, 135–9, 156–9 ; Simone Maiolo, *Dies Caniculares*, coll. ii, ed. 1691, pp. 28–9.

[102] *Opera*, Quaracchi, tom. ii (1885), pp. 204–5. " Daemonum consilium uel auxilium non potest requiri absque peccato."

[103] *Compendium Mal.*, ii, i, Eng. tr., p. 84.

[104] " Nudata tota." *De Miraculis Rerum Naturalium*, Antuerpiae, 1560, lib. ii, xxvi.

[105] Ed. Buecheler, Berolini, 1895 (Iterato), 61 and 62, pp. 40–1.

[106] " Michael in lupum transfigurabatur uestitus, Petrus uero exutus." De. Mag. Poenis. vi, xiv. *Opera Omnia*, Amstedolami, 1660, p. 497.

[107] *Tableau de l'Inconstance*, Paris, 1613, livre iv, p. 290.

[108] Folio, Bononiae, 1637, lib. i, cap. vi, p. 149.

[109] Eng. tr., p. 84.

[110] Eng. tr., pp. 146, 150–1, and 69.

[111] *Inconstance*, u.s., p. 295.

[112] Ed. folio, Moguntiae, 1603, p. 164.

[113] Francofurti, 1607, p. 154.

[114] p. 322.

[115] Virgil, folio, 1697, pp. 39–40, ll. 135–144.

[116] p. 85.

[117] viii, 2, pp. 219–20.

[118] In the " Refutation des Opinions de Iean Wier ", which forms an appendix to the *Demonomanie*, Bodin snibs Weyer for following " l'opinion de *Baptiste Porta* Italien, le louant bien fort ", and describing at length the witch-ointment. He speaks chidingly of " l'Italien Baptiste " and " son liure de la Magie, c'est à dire Sorcellerie ", ed. 1580, pp. 231–2. In livre iv, ch. 5, Bodin calls upon the magistrates " de brusler sur le champ tous liures de magie " (p. 208).

[119] *Opera*, Amstedolami, 1660, pp. 222–5.

[120] Folio, Basileæ, 1557, p. 500.

[121] *Examen*, Eng. tr., ch. xxvi, pp. 77–80 : *Whether Witches Afflict with Words*.

[122] Vair, *De Fascino*, Paris, 1583, lib. ii, cap. xi, pp. 187–160. Bodin, *Demonomanie*, ed. 1580, livre ii, ii, pp. 60–2. Speaking of muttered spells he justly says : " Et ne se peut faire par la vertu des paroles . . . mais le Diable est le seul autheur, & ministre de telles fascinations."

[123] 1872, p. 406.

[124] Col. Agrippinae, 1594, p. 282.

[125] *Historia Septentrionalis*, Romae, 1555, xviii, cxlv, p. 643. But in the English translation which I quote in the text, folio, 1658, book xviii, chapter xxxii (p. 193). The English version is an abridgement (in parts) of the original, and when citing this for the flavour of the phrase sake, I have compared the translation with the original, and amended or added as necessary.

[126] See Montague Summers, *History of Witchcraft*, London, 1926, ch. iii, pp. 82–3.

[127] *Compendium*, Eng. tr., book i, ch. vi, pp. 18–19. Also Sinistrari,

Demoniality, Eng. tr. by Montague Summers, 1927, pp. 8–9, with notes pp. 104–5.

[128] *Dæmonomagia*, 1607, p. 155.

[129] *Dialogue de la Lycanthropie*, 1596, p. 88.

[130] Ed. ut cit. sup., folio, 1603, lib. ii, q. xviii, p. 165.

[131] *Restitution*, p. 287.

[132] Ut cit. sup., p. 164.

[133] *Dæmonomagia*, 1607, p. 153.

[134] *Tableau de l'Inconstance*, livre iv, p. 310, and pp. 260–1.

[135] Eng. tr., chapter xlvii, p. 150.

[136] *Otia Imperialia*, ed. Felix Liebricht, Hanover, 1886. Tertia Decisio, cxx, pp. 51–2.

[137] Various legends concerning the wolf will be found in De Gubernatis, *Zoological Mythology*, 1872, vol. ii, ch. xi, pp. 141–152.

[138] " Potum in ursinam rabiem agat." *Naturalis Historia*, apud Hackios, 1669, t. i, p. 586.

[139] *De Maleficio Affectis*, iv, cap. xxiii, 6. *Opera Omnia*, Amstedolami, 1660, p. 386.

[140] English tr., ut cit., p. 154.

[141] *Malleus*, part ii, qn. 2, ch. 4.

[142] *Speculum Naturale*, ii, cap. cix. Folio, Venice, 1591, tom. i, p. 26.

[143] Ut cit. sup., pp. 51–2.

[144] J. Bonnafoux, *Legendes et Croyances Superstitieuses de la Creuse*, Guéret, 1867, p. 27.

[145] J. F. Bladé, *Contes et Proverbes Populaires recueillis en Armagnac*, Paris, 1867, p. 51.

[146] Paul Sebillot, *Le Folk-lore de France*, Paris 1904–7, t. ii, p. 205 ; Wigrin de Taillefer, *Antiquités de Vésone*, i, p. 250 ; J. L. M. Noguès, *Les Mœurs d'autrefois en Saintonge et en Aunis*, Saintes, 1891, p. 233 ; Americ-Jean-Marie Gautier, *Statistique du département de la Charente-Inférieure*, La Rochelle, 1889, p. 235.

[147] A. de Chesnil, *Usages de la Montagne-Noir*, p. 374.

[148] J. Bonnafoux, *Legendes* . . . ut cit., p. 28.

[149] Part ii, qn. 2, ch. 4, Eng. tr., pp. 173–5.

[150] Migne, *Patres Latini*, tom. iii, 1198.

[151] Ibid., tom. iv, 574–5.

[152] " Stephanus Baluzius Tutelensis in unum collegit, magnam partem nunc primum [anno 1677] edidit, reliquas emendauit."

[153] For other similar details and traditions see Jacob Grimm, *Teutonic Mythology*, tr. from the 4th edition by J. S. Stallybrass, 4 vols. : vol. iii (1883), pp. 1093–9 ; and also for further notes, vol. iv (1886), pp. 1629–30.

[154] *Examen*, xlvii, Eng. tr., p. 151.

[155] This is a conflation of three lines from Ovid, *Metamorphoseon*, i, l. 239, l. 234, and l. 235. In the last line, " et nunc quoque sanguine gaudet " has been changed to " et fuso iam sanguine gaudet ".

[156] *Tableau de l'Inconstance*, livre iv, p. 296.

[157] Ibid., p. 309.

[158] Ibid., p. 309.

[159] See Montague Summers, *The History of Witchcraft*, 1926, pp. 70–5 and p. 89.

[160] " A man whose eyebrows meet . . . may be marked by this sign either as a werewolf or a vampire." Tylor, *Primitive Culture*, 4th ed., 1903, vol. ii, p. 193. Jacob Grimm (ut sup.) quotes Thiele, i, 133, to the effect that if a man's eyebrows meet over his nose, although retaining a human shape by day, at night he will become a wolf. See also C. G. Seligmann, *Der böse Blich*, Berlin, 1910, i, 75 ; and Blaer, *Das Altjüdische Zauberwesen*, Strassburg, 1898, p. 153.

[161] 1926, vol. i, chapter 8, p. 419.

[162] Grimm, op. cit., vol. iv, p. 1630.

[163] *Tableau de l'Inconstance*, livre iv, p. 323.

[164] *Opera Omnia*, folio, Venice, 1606, p. 117. " Nam quamuis magica

arte fiant multa signa, uel per medium naturae, quod possunt angeli, sed etiam dæmones, sola tamen illa miracula dicenda sunt quae operatur Uerbum per ministeria angelorum, quibus hoc in priuilegium praestari dignatur, aut per Sanctos, in quibus Idem."

[165] Job, ii, 6.

[166] *In Primam Secundae S.*, *Romae*, folio, Venice, 1589, p. 962. Art. Decimus, Quaest. 113 ; v ; *De iustificatione impii*. For Conrad Koellin see Qúetif and Echard, *Scriptores Ordinis Praedicatorum*, folio, Paris, 1721, tom. ii, p. 100.

[167] *Demonomanie*, 1580, p. 241.

[168] Eng. tr., p. 123.

[169] *Demonolatry*, book ii, ch. 5. Eng. tr., 1930, pp. 108–114.

[170] Part ii, qn. ch. 8, Eng. tr., p. 123.

[171] *Examen*, c. xlvii, Eng. tr., p. 146.

[172] *Compendium*, book i, ch. xiii, Eng. tr., p. 51.

[173] Ibid.

[174] *L'Incredulite Sçavante*, Lyon, 1678. Discours xxx and Discours xxxi, pp. 890–908.

[175] Eng. tr., p. 73.

[176] *L'Incredulite Sçavante*, Lyon, 1678, p. 900.

[177] *Compendium*, book i, ch. xiii, Eng. tr., p. 51.

[178] *Examen*, ch. xlvii, Eng. tr., pp. 146–151.

[179] Bodin, *Demonomanie*, II, vi.

www.ingramcontent.com/pod-product-compliance
Lightning Source LLC
Chambersburg PA
CBHW060407030726
47497CB00003B/872